Tanner Was Unsaddling His Horse When Maggie Suddenly Appeared At His Side.

"You know, I'd like a chance to sit down and talk to you, uninterrupted," she said.

Tanner stepped back. Her nearness was still capable of unnerving him. "No, I—"

"We haven't really had a chance since I moved in. You've been so busy, and so have I. But tonight—"

"I can't!" Tanner said desperately. "I've got to... got to...muck out the barn."

"I'll help you muck out the barn later."

"No!"

Maggie cocked her head. "You know, Robert," she said, one corner of her mouth lifting as she looked straight at him, "the way you're constantly trying to avoid me, I could get the impression that you're afraid of me."

"I am not afraid of you!"

Her smile never wavered. "Really? Then prove it...."

Dear Reader,

There's so much in store for you this month from Silhouette Desire! First, don't miss *Cowboys Don't Cry* by Anne McAllister. Not only is this a *Man of the Month*— it's also the first book in her CODE OF THE WEST series. Look for the next two books in this series later in the year.

Another terrific miniseries, FROM HERE TO MATERNITY by Elizabeth Bevarly, also begins, with *A Dad Like Daniel.* These delightful stories about the joys of unexpected parenthood continue in April and June!

For those of you who like a touch of the otherworldly, take a look at Judith McWilliams's *Anything's Possible!* And the month is completed by Carol Devine's *A Man of the Land,* Audra Adams's *His Brother's Wife,* and *Truth or Dare* by Caroline Cross.

Next month, we celebrate the 75th *Man of the Month* with a very special Desire title, **That Burke Man** by **Diana Palmer.** It's part of her LONG, TALL TEXANS series, and I know you won't want to miss it!

Happy reading!

Lucia Macro
Senior Editor

Please address questions and book requests to:
Silhouette Reader Service
U.S.: 3010 Walden Ave., P.O. Box 1325, Buffalo, NY 14269
Canadian: P.O. Box 609, Fort Erie, Ont. L2A 5X3

ANNE
McALLISTER
COWBOYS DON'T CRY

SILHOUETTE *Desire*®
Published by Silhouette Books
America's Publisher of Contemporary Romance

SILHOUETTE BOOKS

ISBN 0-373-05907-8

COWBOYS DON'T CRY

Printed in U.S.A.

ANNE McALLISTER

was born and raised in California, land of surfers, swimmers and beach-volleyball players. She spent her teenage years researching them in hopes of finding the perfect hero. It turned out, however, that a few summer weeks spent at her grandparents' in Colorado and all those hours in junior high spent watching Robert Fuller playing Jess Harper on "Laramie" were formative. She was fixated on dark, handsome, intense, lone-wolf types. Twenty-six years ago she found the perfect one prowling the stacks of a university library and married him. They now have four children, three dogs, a fat cat and live in the Midwest (as in "Is this heaven?" "No, it's Iowa.") in a reasonable facsimile of semiperfect wedded bliss to which she always returns—even though the last time she was in California she had lunch with Robert Fuller.

Cowboys Don't Cry is the first in a three-book series about the Tanner brothers, the oldest of whom, Anne is quick to point out, bears absolutely no resemblance to anyone else named Robert she's ever met. In the coming months, watch for Luke's story in *Cowboys Don't Quit* and Noah's in *Cowboys Don't Stay*.

For Patricia Smith and Luigi Bonomi,
editors who make writers glad to write

For Walter C. Perkins,
1932-1993,
my first cowboy hero

One

Tanner could hear them arguing even as he came along the side of the barn.

"He can't."

"Can so."

"No way."

"Yessir."

"No disrespect, Ev," he heard Bates say earnestly in his polite, college-boy voice. "Tanner's the best at breaking broncs in these parts, no two ways about it. But I don't reckon even he could stay on this one."

As he rounded the corner, Tanner saw old Everett Warren spit in the dust, then aim a glare at the younger cowboy. "Shows what you know."

"Yeah," a third, much higher voice chipped in, and Billy, Ev's nine-year-old grandson, swung up on the corral fence. "Tanner can do anything."

Tanner grinned a little at the boy's confidence in him. In fact, he hoped Billy was right. If he was, then everything would work out fine when he had to deal with his new boss this afternoon.

But before he had a chance to start thinking about that again, he saw Bates shake his head. "Not this mare," he said, nodding at the one whose bridle he held.

She was the sweetest-looking jet black beauty Tanner had ever seen. The upcoming interview faded from his mind at the sight of her. Talk about prime horseflesh.

Tanner stopped and simply admired the mare as she fidgeted, stamping, tossing her head and shimmying as Bates spoke.

"'Course he can. Can't you?" Ev added, when he turned and saw Tanner coming their way.

"You can ride her, can'tcha, Tanner?" Billy demanded.

Tanner didn't say anything, just stood considering her, tempted.

Ev grinned. "Sam Gallagher just brought her over. Says ain't no one can stay on her at his place."

"Plenty of guys have tried," Bates put in quickly. "Gibb got bucked off last week. Didn't last five seconds. Walker and Del Rio tried, too, and both of 'em bit the dust. Not surprising really, those two . . . but Gibb, he's dynamite."

"He ain't Tanner," Billy said stoutly.

"Ain't nobody better'n Tanner." Ev nodded emphatically, chewed and spat again. He looked at Tanner, his pale blue eyes clear and bright. "Show him."

Tanner cocked his head. "Just like that?"

"You've rid your share," Ev reminded him.

But that had been a while back. He was thirty-four now and occasionally aware after a long day in the saddle of his thrice-broken ribs, a shattered ankle, a lumpy collarbone, a shoulder with a permanent tendency toward dislocation and the two pins still residing in his left knee.

Still, she *was* a beauty. And there was nothing in the world like pitting your strength against so much sheer energy, nothing that could compare with settling down onto a half a ton of twisting, surging animal. It felt as if you had the world by the tail.

Even so, Tanner hesitated. He looked with longing at the ebony mare, feeling the weight of his responsibilities pressing down on him as he did so.

"What good's a dead foreman, I'd like to know?" Abigail had scolded last spring when he'd hit the dust, concussed, after being thrown by a frisky bay. "I don't pay you to break horses or bones!"

"I'm fine," Tanner had assured her, swallowing the dirt in his mouth and wiping a streak of blood off his lip. "Don't fuss."

But Abigail Crumm had loved a good fuss. And when a woman got to be eighty-four, a woman did whatever a woman wanted to do. In this case it was to prevail upon Tanner to stop riding broncs.

"Is that an order?"

Abigail had given a tiny, dry laugh. "Of course not. I'm simply asking, Tanner." She'd slanted him a coy glance, adding in her best quavering old-lady voice, "I do so worry about you, you know."

Tanner had snorted. Abigail had smiled.

He hadn't ridden the bronc. A bad heart had made Abigail vulnerable and Tanner was damned if he was going to be the death of her. She'd had enough to worry about without him.

But now Abigail was gone.

The slight cold she'd brushed off in February had turned into pneumonia the first week in March.

He'd told her to go to the hospital. He'd told her orange juice and afternoon naps weren't enough. But Abigail had ignored him.

"You know horses, Tanner, I'll give you that," she'd said with as much briskness as she could muster. "You're a good cattleman, too. A wonderful foreman. But until you can show me a medical degree, I'll do my own doctoring."

"They got medical degrees in Casper. I'll drive you," he offered almost desperately.

But Abigail had simply smiled up at him from her rocking chair and taken another sip of juice. Outside the wind had rattled sleet against the windowpanes. "No."

"Damn it, you're not going to get well like this!"

"I've had a good life, Tanner. I'd rather die with my boots on like my daddy did than molder away in some hospital room."

"You're not gonna molder, Abigail!"

"No," she said firmly. "I'm not."

She hadn't. But she hadn't survived, either.

Two weeks ago, almost late because he'd had to ride halfway to Hole-in-the-Wall to fix a fence, Tanner had sat slumped in the back pew at her funeral to listen to Reverend Dailey remind everyone what an inspiration Abigail Crumm had always been.

"She went her own way. She did her own thing. At one time or another, she had the cattlemen, the oil men, the sheep men, and the townspeople all mad at her. But there wasn't a more caring person in the whole of Wyoming than Abigail Crumm."

Reverend Dailey's eyes scanned the packed church, looking at all the people whose lives Abigail Crumm had touched. Then he smiled. "Or," he added, "a more surprising one."

At the time Tanner hadn't realized the full import of that statement.

Now he did.

And in a little less than an hour he'd be meeting the biggest one.

He'd been prepared to have Abigail leave the ranch to one of her causes. The good Lord knew she'd had plenty of 'em—all the way from stray cats to homeless children. And Tanner had figured he could handle that. Being foreman with an absentee landlord was the best of all possible worlds. Besides, who else would she leave it to? Ab had no living relatives. As highly as she thought of her old friend Ev, he didn't have the stamina to manage a spread this big, and Tanner knew she wouldn't leave it to him.

In fact, he'd made damned sure she didn't.

"The hell you say," he'd sputtered when she'd told him she was thinking of naming him her beneficiary. "What would you go and do a stupid thing like that for?"

"I trust you, Tanner. You know the ranch better than anyone."

"I know what a load of work it is. You ever see a happy rancher, Abby? 'Course not. They got too many worries to be happy. No thanks. I'm a cowboy, not a rancher. And cowboys don't stay. We're free. No strings attached. I came with my saddle. I'll go with my saddle. That's the way I like it."

"You've been here four years," Abigail reminded him.

"And I can leave tomorrow."

"Do you want to?"

He shrugged, feeling uncomfortable under her speculative blue gaze. "'Course not," he said after a moment. "Not now anyhow. You need me."

She smiled gently. "Yes."

"So—" he shrugged "—I'll hang around awhile. Because I want to. Not because I have to. Don't you go tyin' me down."

Abigail just looked at him for a long moment, so long that Tanner wondered whether she was really seeing him or something else entirely. Finally, she'd nodded. "Whatever you say, Tanner."

When Ev came home and told him over supper what the will said, he found that she'd left him a horse trailer and her two best saddle horses. "Portable assets," she'd called them.

She left the ranch to Maggie MacLeod.

"What the hell's a Maggie MacLeod?" Tanner had asked, taking the cup of coffee Ev handed him. He hadn't had time to go to the reading himself. Cows didn't stop calving just for wills to be read. "Never heard of it."

It sure as hell didn't sound like stray cats. But Tanner didn't really care. One cause was as good as another as far as he was concerned, as long as whoever was in charge stayed out of his way and let him do his job.

"Not a committee," Ev had said. "A woman."

A woman. *One* woman? Tanner frowned. "Just a regular...person, you mean?" Not a cause at all?

"Uh-huh." Ev nodded, grinning.

"What sort of woman?"

"Schoolmarm."

Tanner couldn't believe it. Visions of starchy, desiccated old prunes fogged his mind. Heaven knew he'd had his share of them. All those years and all those classrooms had seemed like some particularly enduring form of torture to Tanner. He couldn't wait to get out.

And now Abby had left the ranch to one?

"Hell and damnation!" He leapt to his feet and stalked around the room.

Ev's grin vanished and he glanced at Billy, then gave Tanner a reproving look. Tanner didn't apologize. He was too busy envisioning what a mess a schoolteacher could make out of the Three Bar C.

"She teaches down in Casper," Billy volunteered. "Third grade. Like Ms. Farragut."

"That's a hell of a recommendation," Tanner muttered. Old Battle-ax Farragut looked like she could freeze a herd of cattle in July, and Tanner knew from what Billy and Ev said that there was only one way to do things as far as she was concerned: Farragut's way. His jaw tightened.

"Ab met her at some soup kitchen," Ev added. "Ladlin' out for the homeless."

"The homeless?" Tanner echoed. He couldn't quite see Farragut doing that. But a do-gooder wasn't much better.

"Swell," Tanner grumbled. "She'll probably want to knit caps for the cattle."

Billy giggled.

"How come Ab never brought her out here?" he muttered, kicking out a chair and dropping into it, scowling.

"She did once or twice. You were gone. Riding fence or feeding cattle. What you were supposed to be doin'," Ev said. "Ab didn't need you to vet her visitors."

"You met her then? What's she like? She live in Casper?" If she had a house and was settled in, that wouldn't be so bad. She could be a landlady from there. Not quite as good as a cause, but...

Ev shook his head. "Nope. And she ain't never been on a ranch before. 'Cept to visit Ab."

Tanner's mouth opened and shut twice before he could say, "You mean Ab went and saddled us with a city slicker?"

Ev shrugged. "She seemed nice enough. Real pleasant, I thought. And, of course, Ab liked her."

"Ab liked more folks than Will Rogers did!"

"Even sour-faced old skunks like you," Ev said easily. He clapped his hand on Tanner's shoulder. "Where's your faith in human nature, boy? Ab wasn't no fool. If she liked this Maggie well enough to leave her the ranch, well, that's good enough for me. I reckon she knew what she was doin'."

Tanner didn't reckon anything of the sort, but he wasn't going to win an argument with Ev about it. Ev had always believed the sun rose and set on Abigail Crumm, and there wasn't any arguing with him. Anyway, a more cheerful thought had just occurred to Tanner.

"She'll probably stay in Casper, then," he said. "City lady like that won't want to be stuck out here. Besides, there aren't many homeless this far out."

But yesterday's mail had brought a letter from Clyde Bridges, Abigail's lawyer, that squelched that hope.

"Miss Maggie MacLeod is looking forward to seeing the Three Bar C." Not even Ms., Tanner had noted grimly. Worse and worse. "She'll be coming on Wednesday. Would you please be available to meet with her at four to discuss her move to the ranch?"

Move to the ranch?

Tanner had stared at the words, willing them to vanish. They hadn't.

He'd shut his eyes and tried once more to imagine the sort of fanatic schoolmarm whom Abigail would've appreciated enough to do something as harebrained as this. Then he tried to imagine such a woman living on the Three Bar C. It didn't bear thinking about.

His only hope was that she'd see it that way, too.

The Three Bar C was not your *House and Garden*–variety ranch. It was damned near a nineteenth-century relic, miles from town in foothills of the Big Horn Moun-

tains. The two-story house was built of pine logs that Abigail's father had cut himself and dragged with his team to
the site. It had four walls, a stone fireplace and character,
but not much else. Even running water and indoor
plumbing had arrived within recent memory.

It was no place for a woman.

Abigail had been born here, of course. But that meant
she'd grown up to it, knew it like the back of her hand.
She'd never had another home.

Miss Maggie MacLeod, whoever she was, had. She
wouldn't belong.

And at four o'clock today, in less than an hour, Tanner
was going to have to convince her of that.

"I dare you," Ev said now.

Tanner blinked, startled back to the present. "What?"

"To ride her."

"Maybe he's got too much sense to risk it," Bates suggested.

Ev shook his head. "Not Tanner."

Tanner gave him a baleful look. "Thanks a lot."

"Just meant you ain't afraid of risks." Ev lifted a brow.
"Are you?"

It was crazy. It was insane. He hadn't ridden an unbro-
ken horse like this mare in over a year. His doctor would
be furious. Ab would be spinning in her grave.

He reached for the reins. He needed the challenge. He
needed the thrill, the physical release that he knew would
come from trying to bring chaos under control. He would
do it; and then he would sort out Miss Maggie MacLeod.

"Awwright!" Billy shouted as Tanner swung up into the
saddle.

In an instant the horse had gathered herself together.
Beneath him, Tanner felt her bunch and thrust, exploding
as she tried to throw this unfamiliar burden from her back.

Flung high and hanging tight, Tanner laughed. He thrust his arm into the air, exulting in her blowup, savoring the surge of powerful energy, the challenge of controlling it, of controlling and taming this little black beauty of a horse.

The landscape blurred around him. Ev and Bates and Billy faded, the fence and the barn evaporated, the car coming over the snow-covered rise disappeared into a haze of winter white and dusty blue.

The world became a swirl of color. All that mattered lay beneath the saddle leather between his legs, in the gleaming sweaty hide of the ebony mare, in the challenge of bringing her under control.

She jumped and snapped, hopped and twisted. Tanner hung on. She raced and shimmied, arched and bucked. Tanner clung.

And then he began to get the rhythm of her. He caught her beat and moved with it. His spine twisted, his knee pained, his head snapped back and his hat flew off.

He stayed on. He anticipated. He compensated. He leaned, arched, dug.

The mare ducked her head, lunging forward, then all of a sudden, jerked back, whipping him upward, unseating him.

He flew. Flipped. Hit.

Hard.

He was in heaven.

Had to be.

Why else, when at last he opened his eyes, would there be an angel with the greenest eyes, the most kissable mouth and the most gorgeous mane of wavy auburn hair he'd ever seen staring down into his face?

He smiled. So there were eternal rewards after all. And hell, he hadn't even had to be a complete saint to get one!

Fuzzy-minded and light-headed, Tanner reached out tentatively to touch her.

"Don't move!"

The sound of her voice was so unexpected that he jerked. It hurt—but no more than reaching out had.

He shut his eyes carefully, trying to get his bearings. Was he in heaven or wasn't he? He didn't think you were supposed to hurt in heaven, but his Sunday-school teachers had never been the best.

Slowly he opened his eyes again, expecting the vision to have vanished.

She was still there, bending even closer now. Her skin looked soft as the petals of Ab's summer roses and there was a faint rosy flush on her cheeks. And God, that mouth! How long had it been since he'd kissed a woman? Tanner swallowed and started to struggle up.

She put out a hand to stop him. "I said hold still. Don't try to get up yet."

She even sounded sort of angelic, her voice was gentle on his ears, caressing almost. Did angels caress? He wanted to ask her, but he couldn't. He still hadn't caught his breath.

All he could do was lie back, give her a muzzy smile and shut his eyes again. His head buzzed.

"He ain't fainted, has he?" This voice was gruff and distinctly non-angelic. *Ev.*

Hell.

Tanner forced his eyes open again. There were other faces crowding into his line of vision now—Ev's, grizzled and worried; Billy's, dismayed; Bates's, resigned.

So much for heaven.

But—he gave his head a small painful shake and tried to focus his gaze—then who was she? Because she still hadn't gone away, this redheaded angel of his.

Tanner levered himself up on his elbows in the mixture of mud and slush and barnyard muck to squint at the woman who was apparently neither a figment of his imagination nor a result of his having fallen on his head.

"Be very careful," she said to him. "You might've broken something."

"Prob'ly did," he said with a gasp, grateful at least that he could finally speak. "Serve me right."

"I told him so," Bates murmured.

"He done better'n Gibb," Billy said stoutly.

"Did," the auburn-haired vision corrected absently.

And hearing her, Tanner moaned.

"What's wrong?" she asked him quickly.

"*You're* the schoolteacher?" He couldn't believe it and knew at the very same moment it was dead-certain true.

His former angel smiled. "That's right. I'm Maggie MacLeod." She held out her hand to him.

He didn't take it. He'd probably have pulled her right down into the muck if he had. Besides, his own were jammed deep in muddy gloves and he wasn't taking them off for the sake of politeness.

Anyway, he didn't want to shake hands with her.

Not just for one reason now, but for a multitude.

This was his new boss? The proper lady schoolteacher? The boot-faced drill sergeant he'd been expecting?

They sure as hell weren't making schoolteachers the way they used to. So much for battle-axes like old Farragut.

But in her way, this one was far worse. She was the prettiest damned woman he'd seen in a month of Sundays. And he was lying flat on his back in the mud in front of her! Suddenly Tanner was burning with embarrassment.

Gritting his teeth, he got to his feet. He would have fallen flat again if Ev and Bates hadn't grabbed him and hauled him up unceremoniously between them.

Being vertical wasn't as much of an advantage as he'd hoped. Maggie MacLeod was almost as tall as he was. The top of that beautiful head of hair was exactly at his eye level. He shook Ev and Bates off and planted his feet squarely.

"You're early," he accused.

"A little." She didn't apologize. But she did smile. And he couldn't help it—it still looked like an angel's smile. There was even a very tiny, very kissable dimple just to the side of her mouth. "I didn't know how long it would take to get here," she was saying when he jerked his attention back to her words. "Some of the gravel roads aren't the best this time of year, you know. I did better than I expected."

And worse than he had hoped.

Tanner grunted. He reached up, intending to jerk his hat down and scowl at her from beneath the brim in the fierce, intimidating look he used whenever he wanted to exert his authority.

His head was bare. He could see his hat lying in the mud clear on the other side of the corral. He swallowed a curse. His hair tangled damply across his forehead and he couldn't even shove it back without making himself a bigger mess than he already was. His fingers flexed and tightened in frustration.

Maggie MacLeod was still smiling, but was also looking at him a little doubtfully. "I have an appointment with Miss Crumm's foreman. Someone called—" she hesitated "—Tanner?"

"That's him," Billy said brightly, poking Tanner in a very sore rib just in case she hadn't already guessed his identity.

Her smile faded momentarily and Tanner felt a split second's hope that she'd take off running in the other direction. Or that maybe, if she wasn't a part of his dream, he was a part of hers and any minute they'd both wake up.

But, Maggie MacLeod said briskly "So it is." She started to offer him her hand again, took a look at the mud and stuffed her fingers into the pocket of her trousers. "Well, it's nice to meet you at last." She waited, expecting a response, apparently.

"Yeah, you, too," Tanner managed after a moment.

"You didn't come to the lawyer's office, I don't believe?"

"Had work to do. Ranch doesn't run itself."

"Yes, that's what Mr. Warren said. Is it—" she hesitated again "—*Mr.* Tanner or..."

"Just Tanner," he said flatly. He glanced at Ev almost desperately. "What time is it?"

"Almost 3:15."

"Our appointment was for four," he said to Maggie.

"Yes, but—"

Tanner jerked his head in the direction of the ranch house. "You can wait in there. I'll be up at four." Surely he could get his act together in half an hour.

Turning on his heel and thanking God his knee didn't go right out from under him, he stalked across the corral, snagged his hat and continued on toward the ebony mare.

"Come on, sweetheart," he said, reaching for the reins again. "You an' I got some work to do."

She didn't wait "in there." She stayed right where she was. She went only so far as to scramble up onto the top rung of the corral fence and settle herself next to Billy. And there she stayed, watching his every move.

He ignored her.

He climbed back into the saddle and put her right out of his head. He didn't even notice her gasp when the mare shot up into the air and twisted so that he nearly fell off. He didn't pay a bit of attention to her rapt gaze or the way her head moved to watch as he and the mare plunged from one end of the corral to the other. He hardly saw the way she flipped her long red hair back out of her face when the wind whipped it around, or the way she winced and sucked in her breath when he got thrown to the ground.

He got thrown three more times.

He could've got thrown a hundred and he wouldn't have given up. Hell, it wouldn't have mattered if the mare had broken every damned bone in his body and killed him in the process.

He wasn't quitting in front of Maggie MacLeod.

Still, each time he hauled himself out of the mud, his shoulder seemed a little less stable and his leg was worse. His ribs began to feel as if the mare had done a tango on them. And the last time he landed, he bit his tongue so hard that he could still taste the blood. Gritting his teeth, Tanner staggered to his feet and headed over to where Ev held the horse.

"You don't have to do this," Bates said quickly.

Tanner took the reins. "Yes, I do."

"Not 'cause of what I said," Ev said quickly. "I didn't mean for you to kill yourself."

"I'm fine."

"'Course you are. That's why you're limping an' spittin' blood."

Tanner ignored him, still not glancing at the woman on the fence, yet feeling her eyes on him anyway as he swung once more into the saddle.

Blessedly, the mare was as tired as he was. And this time when he got on her back, she did nothing more than give a couple of half-hearted bucks and a shimmy, then she tossed her head and trotted easily around the corral.

"I tol' you so," Billy crowed. Ev grinned, and Bates looked downright impressed.

Tanner couldn't tell what Miss Maggie MacLeod thought. She didn't say a word and he didn't glance her way. It was all he could do to keep from grimacing at every step the mare took. But he rode her around twice more before he urged her over to the far side of the corral and slid carefully out of the saddle.

Leaning against her, he talked to her, soothing her. She needed that, but so did he, in order to give his trembling, aching leg time to adjust once more to solid ground. Even so it damn near buckled when he took his first step.

"You okay?" Ev asked him.

"Swell." He winced, then walked gingerly, masking his limp with as much nonchalance as he could muster as he led the mare toward the barn.

He waited until he got there and could support himself with his hand against the doorframe before he turned and faced Maggie MacLeod.

He glanced at his watch. It was quarter to four. "I'll be up to the house as soon as I've got her settled. Put on the coffee and we'll talk."

Tanner had never played football, but he didn't have to be a quarterback to know that there was truth in the cliché about the best defense being a good offense. He also knew he needed one. Bad.

"She's really beautiful, ain't she?" Billy asked him, skipping along ahead of Tanner, but glancing back at Maggie, who was walking toward the house.

Tanner didn't have to glance back. Imprinted on his mind from a mere few seconds of watching her was the way she moved. He could shut his eyes right now and still see the feminine sway of her hips in those soft, elegant trousers. He swallowed and brushed past Billy into the bunkhouse. "She's all right," he allowed.

Bates, following along after him, snorted. "All right? She's a fox."

"You don't have to drool," Tanner snapped.

"Hey—" Bates lifted his hands and stepped back "—I was only saying. I'm not poaching." He looked Tanner up and down. "You want her, you can have her."

"What the hell would I want her for?" Tanner grumbled. He pulled off his shirt, wincing as his shoulder popped.

Bates grinned. "What would you want her for? You don't know? Hell, Tanner, I knew you were a little slow sometimes, but I thought even you knew what to do with a woman!"

"Shut up, Bates," Tanner said with a geniality he didn't feel. He stripped off his shirt and yanked a clean one out of the closet. Most of his clothes were up at the house, since he'd moved up there last year. Now he was glad he kept a few things down here. He padded into the bathroom and turned on the shower, then paused to consider his face in the mirror.

He was grimy and sweaty and filthy. Under the dirt he could see the beginnings of a bruise on his cheekbone where one of the stirrups had caught him when he was flying through the air. And there was a cut over his left eye, but the blood had pretty much dried. The cut inside his mouth wasn't worth worrying about.

He turned his head, looking at his face dispassionately. He wasn't what any woman would call really handsome, though they didn't exactly run in the other direction. He had a lean face, weathered. His eyes were blue and deep set beneath dark brows. He needed a shave. He scowled at his reflection.

He frowned too much, Abby told him. "Smile, Tanner," she was always telling him. He made himself smile. It could have been worse.

Once he got the mud off and the whiskers, he'd clean up pretty good.

Of course, he needed a haircut. He rarely bothered to get his thick, shaggy hair trimmed. There were always more important things to do whenever he got to town. Maybe he could yell for Ev and see if the old man wanted to take a few whacks. And then Maggie wouldn't think—

Whoa!

He stopped dead, staring at himself in the mirror, making himself run that thought through his head again. *Maybe Maggie wouldn't think—*

Again he stopped.

Finish it, he commanded himself.

Maybe Maggie wouldn't think he was such a bum.

Damn it, what did he care what Maggie MacLeod thought of him?

He flipped the shower off again, instead simply ducking his head under the tap of the sink, scrubbing his face and hair until most of the grime was gone.

He took an old razor out of the medicine chest, studied his whiskery cheeks, then put the razor back again.

There was no reason to spruce himself up for Maggie MacLeod. He was working for her, not courting her, for God's sake.

Tanner hadn't courted anyone in years. Wasn't ever going to again!

The very notion that he might, even in his subconscious, have considered it, infuriated him. Scowling, he stalked back into the other room.

"Hand me that shirt," he said to Billy.

"I thought you were going to— Aren't you going to—?" Bates glanced toward the shower, then back at Tanner's still-sweaty torso. He shut his mouth.

Tanner buttoned the shirt and jammed it down into his jeans. If the faint odor of horse and mud clung to him, that was too damn bad. If Maggie MacLeod thought she was going to like ranch living, she'd better get used to the smell.

He shoved away the thought that Abigail would have had his hide if he'd ever dared show up at the house like this. The Three Bar C might not be the center of the civilized world, but Abigail had been a hat-and-gloves-type lady.

Tanner had known better than to take his sweat-and-mud-stained body anywhere near her. She'd demanded civilization even from the likes of him.

But Maggie MacLeod wasn't Abigail.

She was a thorn in his side and he was going to do his damnedest to get rid of her.

He was glad he'd stayed awake all last night preparing a series of rational arguments that would convince a dried-up, prune-faced schoolmarm that the Three Bar C was no place for a lady. He prayed to God the same arguments would work as well on Miss Maggie MacLeod.

As he strode across the yard and climbed the stairs to the porch, the wind shifted and he caught a good whiff of the corral smell he was bringing in with him.

Maybe he wouldn't need rational arguments at all, he thought with a grin. Maybe just one look and one deep breath would be enough to send her packing.

A guy could hope.

Two

With his hand on the doorknob, Tanner hesitated, wondering if she'd expect him to knock. Did she know that he and Ev and Billy had been sharing the house with Abigail since last summer?

But before he could decide what to do, he heard her call out, "Come in."

She was sitting in Abigail's rocking chair near the fireplace, and while he'd been concentrating on walking without a limp, now he stopped dead, jolted at the sight.

No one ever sat in that chair except Abby.

He opened his mouth to protest, then realized that it didn't matter anymore. Abby wouldn't care.

Abby had wanted it this way, he reminded himself grimly.

And the worst thing about it was Maggie MacLeod looked comfortable there, as if she belonged.

She looked warm and cozy. Settled. His jaw tightened.

Someone—her probably, for Tanner couldn't imagine anyone else having done it—had laid another log on the fire, and now it burned cheerfully, crackling and snapping, just the way Abby had always liked it. On the end table next to her she had a tray with a coffeepot, mugs and cookies.

Where'd she get cookies? Tanner wondered irritably.

He took off his hat, rolling the brim between his palms, and stood scowling at her. Maggie got to her feet and came toward him, smiling. Without her coat on, he could see that her figure was as every bit as angelic as her face. Those elegant trousers that had swayed when she walked were a dark green, soft wool. She wore an off-white sweater with a sort of loose rolled collar that offered glimpses of the lightly freckled creamy skin of her neck. And below that her breasts lifted the soft angora of the sweater—

"—glad you survived your encounter with the bronc."

He blinked, jerking his gaze away from her breasts, swallowing hard and discovering that she was once more offering him her hand and waiting expectantly.

A tide of hot blood coursed up his neck. She must think he was an idiot! He loosed his fingers from the brim of his hat and took the hand she offered him.

Her grasp was firm and warm and soft. *Womanly skin.* He couldn't remember the last time he'd felt skin that silky. It made him more aware than ever of the rough calluses on his own. He drew his hand away quickly and stuffed it in his pocket.

"Just part of the job," he said gruffly.

The skeptical look she gave him made him shift from one foot to the other uncomfortably. But then she smiled and shrugged. "I'm sorry you felt you had to hurry."

Her gaze flicked from his stubbled cheeks to his dirty jeans and he saw immediately the interpretation she had put on his lack of grooming.

"I didn't hurry! I mean I—" Damn it, he might've known she'd miss the point!

Showing up unshaven and reeking of a barnyard didn't mean he was dying to be at her beck and call, but he could hardly say that. His scowl deepened. He crushed the brim of his hat with his hands.

"In any case, I appreciate your taking the time for me, Mr. . . ."

"It's not Mr., ma'am. I told you, just Tanner."

"Is that your first name, then?"

"No."

She smiled and he saw that damned dimple again. "What's your first name?"

He frowned. "Robert."

It sounded odd to say it, to hear it said aloud. He'd been Tanner for so many years that he could hardly remember being anyone else. Even his brothers called him Tanner. His father hadn't, of course. But Bob Tanner, Sr., when he'd called his eldest boy anything, had simply called him "Son." Certainly no one had called him Robert for years—not even . . .

Deliberately he shut off the thought. No one had called him Robert since his mother, in fact, and she'd died when he was seven.

Maggie MacLeod smiled at him now and took his arm. "Come and sit down, Robert."

He might've known.

"Everyone calls me Tanner, ma'am," he corrected her firmly, but he had the feeling she didn't hear him.

He sat down, not on the sofa as she indicated, but on the hearth, leaning back against the rough stone and watching her warily while she poured two cups of coffee. His arm still tingled where she'd touched him. Surreptitiously he rubbed it against his side.

Maggie looked up. "Is something wrong?"

He colored furiously and sat up ramrod straight. "No, ma'am."

She nodded easily. "If you're not comfortable there, you might prefer the sofa," she suggested.

"Here's fine." It was as far away from her as he could get.

"Suit yourself."

Hell, if he could do that, he wouldn't be here at all. He twisted the brim of his hat harder.

"Do you take milk or sugar?"

"Black. Please," he added when the one word sounded too abrupt.

Maggie got up and handed him one of the mugs, then added a dollop of milk to her own, stirring it in. She settled back into Abigail's chair and lifted the mug to her lips. She sipped, swallowed, then smiled at him. He tried not to notice.

"I'm so glad to talk to you at last. I know we haven't met, but I feel like we have. Abby told me so much about you."

"She did?" Swell. He wished Abby had told him anything at all about her. Then maybe he wouldn't be feeling quite so much as if he was walking on quicksand right now.

He wanted to be able to plunge right into his arguments for her staying in Casper. But while he could envision saying them firmly and forcefully to a battle-ax like old Farragut, somehow with Maggie his mouth felt dry and the words wouldn't form.

He took a swallow of coffee and studied Maggie MacLeod the way he sized up an unknown, untried horse.

But the ebony mare was a lot easier to figure out than Maggie was.

She wasn't what he'd expected. Some ancient, do-gooding loony wouldn't have surprised him. Hell, it was what he'd hoped for. Maybe Maggie was a do-gooding loony. He'd just never met one who looked quite like her before.

He wondered for the first time just what Abigail had had in mind when she left Maggie the ranch. The old lady had always been a doer, a manipulator, a campaigner with a million causes.

Just because she was only one woman didn't mean Maggie wasn't one of them, Tanner realized. What sort of cause was Maggie MacLeod?

But studying her more closely didn't provide any answers. All it did was make him aware of how damned attractive she was and how, even now, his body responded to her.

For years Tanner had been able to take women or leave them. Mostly he did the first, then the second.

Except if they looked like gentle, love-you-forever types like Maggie MacLeod—then he took off running and never looked back.

Which is what he ought to be doing right now, he thought grimly. Except he couldn't. He'd promised Abby he'd stay for awhile and help the new owner make the transition.

He hadn't thought anything of it when he'd made the promise. And if it made Abby rest easier, what was the problem?

Trust Abby.

"What'd she say about me?" he asked at last. He didn't know where else to start, and it might help if he knew what sort of nonsense Abby had filled her head with.

"How much she depended on you," Maggie replied. She leaned back in the rocker and set it in motion gently, still smiling at him. "She said you were the reason she was able to keep the ranch going, that if you hadn't been here over the last few years, she would have had to move to town. She said you worked day and night, that you helped Mr. Warren keep the house repaired, the truck running and the cattle fed. She said you were a good horseman." Her smiled widened slightly. "She said you were a wonderful influence on Billy. The kindest, most thoughtful, most responsible man she'd ever known."

Tanner ducked his head, discomfited by the praise. "Yeah, well, I guess I'm a regular paragon, aren't I?" he muttered gruffly.

Maggie laughed. "Abigail certainly seemed to think so."

"She was prejudiced," Tanner said flatly. "Any good hand would do what I do."

"Including almost getting yourself killed on a horse this afternoon?"

"I survived."

"You're still limping."

So he hadn't managed to hide it from her. "No big deal."

"Maybe not. But your survival is a big deal. You die and this place falls apart. I don't know a thing about ranching. Without you, the Three Bar C would be chaos."

"You could find somebody."

"But Abby promised me you."

The simple words hit like a fist in the gut. Maggie herself seemed to realize they might be taken another way, too, for her cheeks took on a deeper hue, and she looked down at her coffee cup. God, she was even more gorgeous when she was embarrassed.

And God help him if he didn't stop thinking that way! "I'm a hired man, not a slave. I can leave whenever I want."

His terseness seemed to take her aback. She looked at him warily. "Is that a threat?"

A promise, he wanted to say. "It's got nothing to do with you. It's me. I don't like bein' tied down."

Auburn brows lifted. "Really? Why not?"

He shrugged, surprised at the directness of her question, unwilling to answer it. "I like my freedom," he said after a moment. "And I'll take it when I'm ready. Meantime I promised Abby I'd hang around for a while to make sure things are running smooth."

"Thank you," she said gravely.

He nodded. "They will, you know. You don't have to supervise. I mean," he went on pressing his point, "you don't have to hang around here, move in. Ev says you've got a place in Casper. Feel free to stay there."

"I don't want to stay there. I like it here. No," she corrected herself, "I love it here."

Tanner stared at her. "It's bleak and cold and lonely as hell."

"It's an hour from Casper."

"The hub of the western cultural world."

"It's a nice town. I've lived in plenty of worse places, believe me."

"You have?" That surprised him.

"My parents are missionaries."

It figured. He groaned inwardly.

"We spent a lot of time living in huts in the middle of nowhere."

"Well, then, you probably want a bit of civilization."

"I want a home."

Her words rocked him. It was as if some long ago bell echoed in his mind. And at the very moment he heard it, he tuned it out.

"You got a home in Casper."

"I have an *apartment* in Casper. I can make the Three Bar C a home. It was Abigail's home," she went on. "That's why she left it to me."

"Huh?" Tanner wasn't following and he was sure he needed to. Things were happening that he didn't like.

"Abigail knew I wanted a home. I've never had one. I've moved all my life."

"So've I," Tanner said. "Nothin' wrong with moving."

"No. Not for some people. But I've done all I want. Now I want someplace to put down roots. To stay. To have a family."

"Casper," Tanner muttered desperately.

Maggie gave him a patient smile. "No. Here. My parents are still abroad, but I have two brothers, one in Colorado and one in Nebraska, and I want to make a home— for myself and for them. Abigail said you had brothers. You must know what I mean." She was looking at him intently.

He knew what she meant, all right. "You don't always get what you want," he said.

"No. But it's no excuse for not trying, is it?" She bit off a piece of cookie and looked right at him.

Tanner's gaze slid away. He shrugged. Stalemate.

"Why do I get the feeling you're trying to get rid of me?"

Because he was, of course. "I'm only trying to do you a favor. The Three Bar C isn't all warm and cheery and fireplaces and stuff. It's muddy and windy and wild and cold, and most times there's not a soul for miles around. There's no people here. Nobody to talk to."

"There's you. And Mr. Warren and Billy."

"We don't count. We're not—not..." he groped for the word " ...conversationalists."

"I don't mind."

I do, Tanner wanted to shout at her. He gulped his coffee, scalded his throat and began coughing. He jumped up and limped around the room. Maggie got up to come after him and pat him on the back.

He brushed her away. "People will talk," he said finally, desperately, when he could speak at last.

"Talk? About what?"

"*Us.* You. Me." Even saying it made hot blood course into his face, and the amused look on her face when she realized what he meant made it ten times worse. "A single woman doesn't live with a bunch of bachelors! It isn't done."

"Well, Abigail certainly didn't tell me everything about you," Maggie said, grinning. "She never once mentioned you were a puritan."

"I'm not a puritan, damn it!"

"Chivalrous, then?"

"I'm not being chivalrous, either! It's common sense. You're a schoolteacher! Schoolteachers got to set a good example, don't they?"

"Yes."

"Well, then—" he took a deep breath "—you'll set a lot better example staying in Casper."

"But I'm not staying in Casper. I believe there's a bunkhouse." She glanced pointedly out the window toward the log building just this side of the barn.

"So? You want us to move out there?"

"Not necessarily. I will."

"You can't do that!"

"Why not? Is that likely to create a scandal, too? Or is someone already living there? A tall, dark, handsome, single ravisher of young women, perhaps?"

Tanner felt as if he was losing his grip. The ebony filly had been a piece of cake compared to Maggie MacLeod. "Of course not. It isn't used now except during round-ups."

"Then what's the problem?"

"You can't let us live here while you move into the bunkhouse! You're the boss, damn it."

"For all the good it seems to be doing me." Maggie laughed, then shrugged. "Well, then, I'll leave where I stay up to you, since you know how things are done in these parts. But try to figure out what to do with me soon, will you, Robert? I'll be moving in on Saturday."

So Tanner moved out.

What the hell else could he do?

He didn't move off the ranch. He didn't hand in his resignation and take off for another state, which is what he'd have preferred. He still had his promise to Abby to consider.

But the very night Maggie announced her intention of moving in, he spent his time, between checks on the cattle, moving into the godforsaken bunkhouse.

It leaked. It was drafty. Ev and Billy thought he was nuts.

"You'll die of pneumonia," Ev told him.

"You'll drown," Billy said.

But Tanner knew better than they did what the dangers in his life were. And he was in greater risk from constant exposure to Maggie MacLeod.

Ev told him he was overreacting. But Ev didn't understand, and Tanner wasn't explaining or even admitting what the problem was.

It was hard enough even admitting the problem to himself.

Maggie reminded him of Clare.

Well, not of Clare herself, really, for Clare had been small and blond and fragile-looking. But of the way he'd felt about Clare.

He'd thought it was a once-in-a-lifetime thing, a product of adolescent hormones, that bolt of instant attraction that could come along and knock a guy on his butt. He wished to God it had been.

There was no way he was going to go through that again.

But if he'd said as much, Ev wouldn't know what he meant. Ev had never heard of Clare. Nor had Bates. Nor Billy. Nor anyone else hereabouts. Not even Abby.

Clare was the part of Tanner's past he tried not to think about. His biggest risk. His greatest failure.

His ex-wife.

Ex-wife. They'd been married such a short time it was hard to even think of her as his wife, let alone his ex. Especially since, for the last fourteen years, he'd tried not to think of her at all.

But for ten months, when she was nineteen and he was barely twenty, he'd been married to her.

And he'd failed her.

She'd been nice about it. She hadn't even blamed him, though God knew she should have. If he'd had a dollar's worth of sense, none of it ever would have happened. It wasn't the dollar's worth of sense he'd needed, he reflected not for the first time, it was a condom.

If he hadn't been such a green kid, if he hadn't been in such an almighty hurry to satisfy his carnal urges, Clare would never have become pregnant. He could remember with absolute clarity the feelings that had hit him the day she told him.

"Pregnant?" He'd almost choked on his disbelief.

Clare nodded, huddled against the door of his pickup. Ordinarily she was pert and pretty, always smiling. Now she looked small and cold and scared.

No colder or more scared than he.

He wanted to ask if she was sure it was his, but one look at her and he knew he couldn't do it. Besides, he thought savagely, if there was the remotest possibility that he wasn't the father, surely Clare would have grasped at it. Damn near anyone would be a better catch than him!

God knew he had enough responsibilities without even thinking about taking on another one. Or two!

His mother had died when he was seven. His father had kept them together just barely, but he'd been killed in a riding accident a year and a half ago. At eighteen, Tanner had gone to work full-time, cowboying on a medium-sized southern Colorado spread while at the same time trying to keep his two hot-headed younger brothers, Luke and Noah, on the straight and narrow.

He wondered for a moment what they'd say when they found out he'd fallen off the straight and narrow himself.

He glanced over at Clare and saw that she was crying now. He felt like crying himself. But cowboys didn't cry. He hadn't, not even at his father's funeral. "Hey," he said softly. "Clare. Hey, don't. Don't. It'll be all right."

She'd looked up, her blue eyes still brimming as they met his. "What do you mean, all right?"

"We'll—" he cast about desperately for an answer, one that would make her tears dry up, that would make things okay, that would make her smile "—get married," he said.

Clare swiped a hand across her eyes. "Do you mean it?" She sniffled and rubbed her nose against her jacket.

"Sure. Why not?" He tried to sound more confident than he felt.

"But I thought—since you've got Luke and Noah—I mean—"

"Luke and Noah will like it," he said. "Somebody littler to tell what to do. They'll be uncles." *And he was going to be a father?* The thought still rocked him. It didn't seem real.

"You're sure?" Clare was blinking now, looking brighter.

"Of course." It might actually be the best thing that could happen, he told himself. Luke and Noah needed more stability than he'd been able to give them. Maybe he and Clare together... "We'll be fine. All of us. We'll have a home."

It was like a dream, airy and insubstantial, but it was all all he had to hang his hopes on. *A home.* Sometime, back before his mother had died, he'd had a home. Warmth. Comfort. Love. A place to come back to, to look forward to.

He smiled at Clare suddenly and leaned over and kissed her. "Yeah. A home."

So they'd married. He'd scraped together enough money to buy a five-times-used old trailer, which his boss let him put out on the land. But there wasn't room enough for the four of them, so he and Clare lived there while Luke and Noah stayed in the bunkhouse up the road, another kindness on McGillvray's part, since both of the boys were in school all day and he didn't need to give them room and board at all.

Tanner had been grateful. He'd actually been glad to have Clare to himself. He'd been smitten with her the first moment he'd seen her, pert and pretty, smiling at customers in Harrison's Hardware Store. She had dreams, plans, hopes, and she shared them all with him. She wanted to go to college, wanted to be a nurse, wanted to see the ocean, to fly in a plane. He'd listened, nodded, smiled, kissed her, kissed her again.

Now that they were married, he wondered if she wanted to be a mother.

The Clare whom Tanner ended up married to wasn't the Clare he'd lusted after since the day they'd met. That one had smiled shyly and clung to his arm when he'd taken her out. That one had kissed him and told him he was her man. This one was sick every morning, cried at the drop of a hat, woke him nightly with her restless turning and insomnia and screamed at him that he was never there when she needed him. He knew a woman's body changed during pregnancy. He knew her moods swung and her desires did, too. But knowing that in theory and understanding in practice were two different things.

He'd tried. God knew he'd tried. But he couldn't be there all the time, could he? He had a job. Money was tight. McGillvray had let several men go. He'd sympathized with Tanner's plight, had praised him for his willingness to accept his responsibilities. He'd kept Tanner on, and now he was depending on him. Hours were long and those sure weren't the days when a cowboy could carry a cellular phone.

As if Tanner's job didn't put enough pressure on his fledgling marriage, Noah was cutting classes to ride broncs. He was only a sophomore, too young by far to drop out of school, and the principal was calling Tanner, the closest thing to a parent Noah had, to convince his brother to shape up.

He could hardly have called on Luke. Luke, who'd always been the closest to their father, was taking Bob Tanner's death hard. "Who gives a damn!" he'd shout whenever Tanner tried to talk to him. He spent most of his nights drinking and fighting and pulling boneheaded stunts on a dare. Five times in their brief marriage Tanner had had to get up in the middle of the night and drive into town to bail Luke out of jail.

No, he wasn't there when Clare needed him.

He wasn't there the day the baby was born.

He couldn't recall now exactly where he'd been. All he could remember was coming back late one April evening, having missed supper by several hours and dreading the tongue-lashing he knew he was going to get the minute he opened the trailer door. Clare wasn't there.

Nor was there any supper waiting, hot or cold. Just silence.

Blessed silence, Tanner had thought at the time.

He remembered guiltily now how he'd basked in it, albeit briefly, before wondering where she'd gone. After a time he'd looked around outside, called her name, then shrugged and put her absence down to the vagaries of pregnancy. Maybe she'd gone for a walk or up to the ranch house to talk to McGillvray's cook.

Tanner went back inside and helped himself to some pork and beans cold, right out of the can. He was just finishing them when there'd come a pounding on the door.

It was Ned Carter, the foreman. Clare had taken sick, he said. McGillvray had driven her to the hospital.

Even then Tanner hadn't thought about her losing the baby. All he'd thought was he hoped she was good and sick if she was bothering McGillvray about it. He owed his boss enough without his wife crying wolf over the least little thing. But he didn't want McGillvray to have to haul her back, too, so he'd borrowed Ned's pickup and driven the thirty miles to the closest hospital.

McGillvray had met him at the door, looking worried and relieved and sad at the same time.

He clapped a hand on Tanner's young shoulder. "I'm glad you're here at last." And before Tanner could apologize to him for whatever inconvenience Clare had put him through, McGillvray said to him, "I'm sorry as hell about the baby."

Tanner said he was sorry, too. What he was was numb. Lost. Dazed.

The baby was dead. His son. McGillvray told him it was a boy. Tanner never saw him. Never even saw Clare that evening. She'd had a hard time, they told him. She'd been sedated, and she was sleeping at last. He didn't wake her.

He went home alone, his mind curiously blank. He woke up in the night and reached for Clare. She wasn't there. He remembered. His son was dead. He tried to summon emotion, pain, hurt. He felt empty. Light, almost. As if he'd escaped a close brush with disaster. It horrified him so much he went into the bathroom and was violently sick.

He never told that to anyone. Certainly he could never tell Clare. He could never explain to her how he felt. He didn't understand it completely himself.

Nor did he understand her.

She cried a little when she got home. Then she just got very remote and quiet and barely spoke to him at all.

She was coping in her own way, he told himself. And he was grateful, because he couldn't help her. Hell, he could barely cope himself.

All he could do was work and ride. He spent more hours than ever before out on the range. He didn't feel good. He didn't feel happy. But he felt better there than facing Clare in the confines of their trailer night after night.

It was sometime in late summer when she told him she'd been talking to Dr. Moberly, the doctor who'd delivered the baby. "He's worried about me," she said. "He says I need to get out of the house, get busy, do something."

He was probably right, Tanner thought, but he didn't know what to suggest. Where the hell was she going to go, stuck out there in the middle of the ranch by herself?

"He thinks I ought to go back to school," she went on.

For the first time since she'd lost the baby, Tanner noticed that there was a little color in her cheeks.

"Swell," he said, feeling the pressure more than ever. "And did he say how we were supposed to afford it? And how you're going to get there? We're thirty miles from the damned school. And tell me, did he suggest what you might study?" He knew he was being sarcastic. He knew he was wrong, that he was hurting her and that he had no right to. He couldn't help it. He'd have liked to go back to school, too. He'd have liked someone to suggest the answer to all his problems.

"He said I could work as a receptionist for him," Clare told him quietly. "And you know I've always wanted to be a nurse."

For a moment Tanner had just stared at her. His questions had been rhetorical. Her answers were not.

"How're you going to work for him," he'd asked finally, "livin' clear out here?"

"I thought," Clare said slowly, carefully, "that I might move to town."

You could have heard a slot machine whir in Las Vegas two full states away. Tanner felt something hard and heavy as lead settle somewhere in his midsection.

He looked at Clare, really looked at her, for the first time in months. She was still beautiful with her porcelain complexion and her fine-boned face. He could still lust after her without even trying. But he hadn't been able to make a home with her. He hadn't been able to give her what she needed. And whatever he might have needed from her, he hadn't found it, either.

"Is that what you want?"

"I want to study nursing, Tanner."

"And . . . us? What about us?"

Helplessly, Clare shrugged.

"Do you want a divorce?"

She twisted her hands. "I . . . think it might be best. I mean, it's not as if we were in . . . I mean, I know you only married me because . . . because of the baby." She swallowed and looked up at him with watery blue eyes and he thought she might start crying again. "I'm tying you down."

He didn't know how long he stood there looking at her, weighing her words and his thoughts.

Maybe he should have argued with her. He didn't. He remembered all those hopes and dreams she'd shared with him, the ones she'd shelved after he'd got her pregnant. He remembered her the way she'd been when he first knew her, happy, smiling. He saw how much she'd changed, how much being married to him had changed her.

"Yeah," he'd said at last.

And no one had come close to tying him down again. Clare had done exactly as she'd said. She'd worked for Russ Moberly as his receptionist. She'd got her nursing degree. And last summer, Noah, who'd spent a night in the town as he traveled between rodeos, reported that she'd married her doctor.

"Got two rug rats already," Noah had said with his customary cheerful insensitivity. "Looks happy. This time I think marriage agrees with her."

Probably it did, Tanner thought. This time she had the right husband. A husband who had it in him to be the sort of man a woman needed, the sort she could depend on.

Not him.

Never him. He wasn't going through that again. Not ever. He'd learned his lesson. And he'd never even been tempted by another marriageable woman.

Until Maggie.

Three

On Saturday morning Tanner stood in the doorway to the barn and watched as Maggie drove up in her little white Ford, pulling a trailer behind.

She was wearing jeans today, and a bright yellow jacket that stopped just before it would have done him the favor of covering the curve of her slender hips. Then she spotted him, smiled and waved, and his gut clenched and his whole body came to attention.

So much for any vague hope that his attraction to her might have been a one-time thing or a result of falling on his head. Tanner lifted his hand, then dropped it abruptly, sucked in his breath and turned away.

Billy and Ev, of course, trooped right out to meet her, beaming and smiling, happy as a couple of cattle in corn. Bates probably would have been there, too, Tanner thought grimly, if he hadn't sent the younger man out at sunup to check on the cattle they were expecting to calve.

He glanced out the door again as Maggie crossed the yard, smiling at Ev and Billy. He heard Billy's high-pitched voice and then Maggie's laugh. The morning breeze whipped through her long red hair.

He wanted to run his fingers through it. He grabbed his saddle and heaved it onto Gambler's back, then drew the cinch up tight, put on the bridle, swung into the saddle and headed out. Billy came running to intercept him. "Maggie's here, Tanner! Ain'tcha gonna help her move in?"

"Nope."

"How come?"

"It's not what she pays me for."

She was standing with Ev on the porch, watching as he approached.

"'Morning," she called.

He gave her a curt nod in greeting and rode on past.

"What'sa matter with him?" Billy asked.

Ev chuckled. "It's spring. The sap is risin'."

"Huh?" said Billy, but Tanner, flushing as he dug his heels into Gambler, knew precisely what Ev meant.

He was a grown man. A foreman, for God's sake.

A responsible, wage-earning adult.

He was also so hungry his stomach thought his throat had been cut. He lay on his bunk, listening to it growl, and reminded himself that he'd missed meals before.

A guy didn't need to eat lunch or dinner every day, he reminded himself for the hundredth time. There wasn't a cowboy alive couldn't stand to shed a few pounds.

That was why he hadn't gone up to the house for dinner, not because he didn't want to run into Miss Maggie MacLeod.

"Yeah, right," Tanner muttered. And if he believed that, next thing you knew he'd be believing that nonsense about lemonade springs and big rock-candy mountains.

All right, so he was avoiding her, had been avoiding her all week. There was nothing wrong with that. He was doing his job the way he was paid to do it, the way he'd always done it. And he didn't need to check with any angel-faced schoolteacher every few minutes for directions. He wouldn't have gone up to see Abby.

Of course, he would have seen Abby every evening at supper, anyway.

All week long he'd managed to avoid Maggie.

"Dietin'?" Ev had asked him, cornering him in the kitchen late one evening when he was ferreting through the cupboards in search of food.

"Calves don't know when it's suppertime," Tanner replied gruffly.

"Reckon not," Ev said. "Maggie's thinkin' you work too hard. Is that what it is?"

"Of course," Tanner said shortly.

"I wondered." But if he looked on speculatively as Tanner carried his sandwiches back to the bunkhouse, at least he didn't say what he was thinking.

But tonight, another Saturday, an entire week from when Maggie'd arrived, Tanner was starving. It was because he hadn't even gotten breakfast, let alone lunch and dinner.

He'd been headed up to the house for breakfast when he'd seen her sitting in the kitchen. Normally on days she drove off to school, he was in and out before she even came downstairs. But this morning, damn it, there she was, puttering around the stove. Ev was nowhere in sight.

She was wearing jeans and a long-sleeved, dark green shirt, and as she moved, Tanner was struck by how long her legs were. They were damned shapely legs, too. He wondered how it would feel to have her legs wrapped around him.

And that was when he knew he couldn't go in for breakfast. He'd taken off for the hills as fast as he could.

Now, fifteen hours later, he was starving. Muttering under his breath, Tanner hauled himself up off the bed and stalked over to the cupboard, jerking it open and ransacking it once more. There had to be a can of beans, a packet of crackers, some beef jerky—anything!—that some long-departed hand had left behind.

He didn't find a crumb.

He hadn't had time all week to go to town and stock up on rations. During calving season, free time wasn't something he had a lot of, and he hadn't dared ask Ev. Ev would've wanted to know why he needed food when they had a kitchen full.

Sighing, he turned on the radio and grabbed the latest *Stockman's Journal*, then dropped down again onto the narrow bunk. He'd read until the lights went out in the house and everybody'd gone to bed.

Then he could sneak up to the house and fix himself a sandwich. Or four.

His stomach growled. "Wait," he told it.

The unexpected knock at the door made him jump. Please God it would be Ev, feeling sorry for him and bearing supper.

It was Maggie.

In one lithe movement he swung his feet to the floor and sat up. "What do you want?"

"I missed you at dinner. Seems I've been missing you all week."

"I wasn't hungry. Besides I've got work to do. Doesn't always fit in with mealtimes."

"Maybe we should change the mealtimes," she suggested. She was wearing her hair piled up on top of her head. Tanner could see the pins. He wanted to remove them.

"What do you want?" he repeated sharply. He got to his feet and strode over to the farthest window before turning around to face her.

"I'd like to go out with you tomorrow."

"Go out with me?" He almost choked on the words.

Maggie's cheeks reddened. "Not on a date," she said quickly. "I just meant . . . Ev says you check the mother cows every morning and I'd like to come."

"No."

His vehemence made her blink. "What do you mean, no?"

"Just what I said. I'm workin' when I'm out there, not guidin' pleasure tours. I don't have time to baby-sit." He folded his arms across his chest and stared at her. His stomach growled.

"It wouldn't be baby-sitting," she said mildly after a moment.

"No? What would you call it?"

"Boss-sitting?"

His teeth came together with a snap and he knew he was trapped. "So you're pullin' rank?"

"Well, saying pretty please didn't seem to be doing me any good," she said with gentle irony. "What time do we start?"

He considered her, took in the heightened color in her cheeks, the sparkle in her big green eyes, the soft thrust of her breasts and the lush curve of her hips that her jeans outlined. *How about right now?* his body suggested to him. Mother cows were the furthest thing from his mind.

"Robert?"

"Damn it! I told you my name is—"

"Tanner. Yes, I know. Very well, *Mis-ter* Tanner, I will be accompanying you in the morning. What time do we start?"

"I'm leaving at sunup."

"I'll be ready." She started toward the door, then stopped and looked back at him. "Abby never said you were surly and hard to get along with, either. Or is it just me?"

Tanner raked his fingers through his hair. "Sorry," he muttered. "It's just there's ... I've ..." But there was no way he could explain. "It's a busy time of year," he muttered at last.

"Well, I don't want to make it worse for you. I just want to know what's going on, to learn all I can about ranching so I won't mess up." She smiled. "Ev says you're afraid I'll try to run the ranch when I don't know what I'm doing. He says you're afraid I'll make a mess of things and cause trouble in your life."

Good old Ev. Tanner's mouth twisted. "Ev talks a hell of a lot."

"He just wanted me to know," Maggie said simply. "He thought it might make things easier between us."

What would make things easier, Tanner wanted to tell her, was if she'd hightail it back to Casper and stay the hell away from him.

"He say anything else?" Tanner asked dryly after a moment.

A smile flickered across her face. "He said you needed a woman in your life."

Tanner gaped at her.

She laughed. "Do you think he's matchmaking?"

"The hell he is!" Tanner slammed his hand against the dresser, furious, hoping she couldn't see the hot blood that had rushed to his face. "I'll kill that nosy old coot. I'll—"

"I get the point," Maggie said lightly. "You have nothing to fear from me."

Oh, didn't he? Tanner wanted to say. He didn't say anything, just folded his arms against his chest once more and prayed she'd leave.

She turned back to the door again, then paused once more and glanced over her shoulder. "Too bad you weren't hungry. We had the most wonderful savory stew with peas and dumplings. It was scrumptious. But perhaps you'll feel more like eating by breakfast time. See you then." He could hear her footsteps on the plank stairs and then she was gone.

Tanner picked up the *Stockman's Journal* and tossed it on the table, flicked off the light and flung himself down on the bed.

His stomach growled.

Tanner got to the house before dawn. He was earlier than usual, but there was a lot to be done. And if he missed Maggie, well, that was just too bad. She'd have to understand.

He looked in the window first, steeling himself in case she was already there. She wasn't. So he breathed easier and opened the door as quietly as he could, hoping not to make noise and wake her. He expected he'd have to fix his own breakfast. Even Ev wouldn't be looking for him this early.

But he found bacon, still crisp and hot, in a covered dish on the back of the stove. In another there were scrambled eggs, and in a third, a pile of warm pancakes. There were hash browns and applesauce, too, as well as the usual pot of strong black coffee.

Tanner breathed it all in, his knees weak from hunger. God bless the old man. He'd really outdone himself, Tanner thought, sitting down and putting it away with relish. "I take back every evil thought I've ever had about you," Tanner said to Ev's absent spirit.

But he apparently didn't want any thanks. He was nowhere around. Just as well, actually, Tanner thought, though it showed a bit more circumspection than was usual for Ev. Tanner had fully expected knowing looks and a blatant wink or two.

He finished off the bacon, eggs and hotcakes. He took a second helping of applesauce and downed another cup of coffee, glancing over his shoulder once or twice toward the stairs, afraid that at any moment Maggie would be coming down them.

She never came.

Probably slept in, Tanner thought with a ghost of a grin. All that business about getting up and coming with him had been no more than mere talk. He shouldn't have spent the night tossing and turning after all.

He carried his dishes to the sink and rinsed them off, then left them on the drainboard for Ev to wash up later. Still no sound of footsteps on the stairs. He felt easier with every passing minute.

He wondered what she'd do if he tiptoed up the steps, stuck his head in her room and woke her. And there was the way to disaster, he told himself sharply. Thinking about Maggie in bed was no way to solve his problem.

He flicked off the light and headed out the door, stuffed his feet into his boots and zipped up his jacket. Then, drawing a deep breath of clean frosty air, he made his way to the barn.

Maggie was already there.

Tanner muffled a curse under his breath and glanced around to check the possibility of getting out without her seeing him. There wasn't one. He sighed, then leaned against the doorjamb and watched.

She had a saddle on Sunny, the ten-year-old sorrel gelding that Abby used to ride, and she held a bridle in her hand, trying to slip the bit into the horse's mouth.

"It won't hurt you," she was saying to the horse. "It's a very humane bit. I checked. Honest. I read up on them just last night."

Tanner shook his head, half amused, half amazed. Maggie approached the horse again, holding the bridle up, grinning widely at him, showing him her teeth, then opening her mouth and clacking her teeth together. "Open up," she said. "Like this."

Sunny pulled back his big horsey lips at her.

"That's it, Sunny," she cooed. "Just like that. And now I'll..." She tried to slip the bit between his teeth. He jerked his head away and clamped down hard. Maggie muttered under her breath.

Tanner tucked his fingers into the front pockets of his jeans. "Why don't you try 'pretty please' on him?"

Maggie spun around to face him, her eyes wide, her cheeks flushed. This morning she had her hair back in what he supposed was meant to be a utilitarian ponytail. But tendrils escaped around her ears and made him want to reach out and touch them. God, it was worse than with Clare. He'd never had to keep his hands in his pockets every minute around Clare.

"I tried that, too, I'm afraid," Maggie said, smiling. "He's as immune as you are. What does work?"

He dragged his mind back from its preoccupation with the physical Maggie MacLeod. "Knowing what you're doing," he said with as much flatness as he could muster.

"I'm sure it would. But Plato once said that we had to do things first without knowing how in order to know how after we've done them."

Tanner heard the faint hint of hurt in her voice and cursed his abruptness. But hell, it was only self-preservation. "You reckon Plato knew a lot about ridin' horses?"

"I don't know. I only know it's all I've got to go on unless you'll show me." She looked at him expectantly in the dim light of the one overhead bulb.

Tanner's jaw tightened. He wanted to say no. He wanted to tell her to take her saddle and her bridle and her whole damn ranch and get out of his life. Or at least he wanted to get out of hers. Why the hell had he made such a promise to Abby anyway?

Finally he strode toward her. "Give it here." He took the bridle out of her hands, careful not to touch her as he did so. Then, quickly and deftly, he slipped the brow band into place, slid the bit between the horse's jaws, adjusted the throat latch and handed her the reins. "There." Then he turned toward his own horse and, with what he hoped was casual indifference, began saddling Gambler.

"Thank you," she said quietly.

"You're welcome." She wasn't, but what was he supposed to say? A glance out of the corner of his eye showed him that Maggie was taking the bridle off Sunny even as she spoke.

"What the hell are you doing?"

"Taking the bridle off so I can practice."

"What?"

"I saw *you* do it. I can't learn unless *I* do it." She got the bridle off again, dropped it, turned it upside down, then right side up, and started again. All the while he stared at her, torn between outrage and bafflement.

This time she got the brow band on all right, but the gelding pulled his head away when she approached him with the bit.

Instinctively Tanner moved to catch the horse's head.

"Don't," Maggie said. He saw the set of her chin, the determination in her eyes, and his arm dropped to his side.

"Fine. Do it yourself."

She tried. She fumbled.

He clenched his fists so as not to reach out and help. "Talk to him, firm like," he told her. "And don't hesitate like that. If you do, he can see you're scared of him."

"I'm not scared of him."

He grinned. "Tell him that, not me."

"I'm trying." Maggie shot Tanner a hard glance, but seeing his grin, she grinned, too. He looked away.

"Come along now, Sunny," she coaxed. "We're in this together, and Robert is laughing at us."

Tanner sucked in his breath.

Maggie grinned at him again, then turned back to the horse. "You don't want to spend the whole morning here, do you? And we will until we get it right."

Then she stuck the bit right between Sunny's teeth. Half triumphant, half amazed, she beamed delightedly. "Oh, you smart horse. I did it!" She turned her face to Tanner's, her cheeks glowing.

She was so radiant he took a step backward. "Like I said," he told her gruffly, "you just gotta be firm. Show him who's boss."

Maggie laughed. "Just you remember that."

Damned right, Tanner thought. As much as he didn't want to think about her being his boss, maybe it was the best thing to think about. Maybe that would keep him from making a fool of himself. Deliberately he turned away and finished saddling Gambler, working swiftly and mechanically, pulling up the strap and tightening the cinch. He put on Gambler's bridle and led him toward the door of the barn. "Come on. Time's wastin'. Can you ride or are you planning to learn that today, too?"

"I can ride."

Tanner gave her a doubtful look, but when she simply lifted her chin and said, "Unless, of course, you'd like to teach me," he got on Gambler and headed west.

"Why aren't you feeding the cattle today?"

"They can manage on their own. There's grass. It's not all snow cover now. See?"

"Do you feed them most days?"

"If there's snow cover."

"How much do you feed them?"

"Too much."

She smiled at him and he felt unaccountably as if he'd said something clever. She'd been plying him with questions since they'd started out. At first his answers had been terse. But at her persistence, he'd expanded on them. And she'd dogged his every step, braving a brisk west wind to peer over his shoulder, poke her nose in everything he did, wanting to know about things he reckoned kindergartners knew the answers to.

But it didn't take him long to see that she didn't.

"How?" she asked curiously. "Why? If she's in labor, why are we leaving her? What are we leaving her for?"

"We'll check on her on the way back," Tanner promised. The cow was just beginning to look like she might deliver. It could be quick; she was a first-time mother. He'd have plenty of time to show Maggie around and come back later and deal with her.

"You're sure she's going to be all right?"

"She'll be fine," he promised.

"When do you plant hay?" she wanted to know.

He was amazed that she listened to his answers. Hung on his every word, damned near, he thought wryly as the morning passed. And he couldn't help feeling flattered, even when he didn't want to be. He explained about the haying, even admitting he'd rather be anywhere else than on the seat of a tractor.

Hell, he thought, disgusted with himself, he hadn't talked that much in years.

He suggested she return to the house when he was done. He wanted to get back to the cow he'd left in the pasture. But Maggie insisted on coming along. They were longer getting back than he'd figured, mostly because he'd been running off at the mouth. And one look told him the cow was going to be the one to pay for it. He dismounted hurriedly, cursing his stupidity under his breath.

"What's wrong?" Maggie climbed down, too.

"I shoulda been here." He hunkered down behind the cow, who was now lying on the snowy ground, exhausted and laboring.

Maggie came to stand behind him. "I thought you said she was all right on her own."

"Was," he muttered. "No longer."

"Can I help?" She knelt down beside him.

"Get out of my way. Go stand over there by the horses." The contraction was passing. He needed to check her now, to see the position of the calf, to see if there was a live calf he might still save. He should've checked her more closely earlier. But he hadn't wanted to make a production of it then. There was something very physical and very basic about labor.

He hadn't wanted to deal with it in front of Maggie. Now he had no choice.

He stripped off his gloves and checked the position of the calf, afraid of what he was going to find and not surprised when he did.

In the best of deliveries the calf's head and front feet were in perfect position for entry into the world. But if this had been one of those, the calf would have already appeared. All Tanner could feel when he tried was a tangle of legs. He muttered under his breath.

"What's wrong?" Maggie was back again, standing right behind his shoulder.

He considered his options. There was a very good chance that, no matter what he tried, neither the cow nor her calf would make it.

She'd been in labor longer than he'd thought. All the natural lubricant he could count on to help ease the calf around and on its way had long since dried up. She wasn't a big cow, either. With some it was easy to turn the calf for delivery. It wouldn't be easy with this one.

A calf leg kicked weakly against his fingers and, as long as there was hope of getting it out alive, he knew he had to try. He straightened up and went to get his rope. Maggie watched him, but she didn't speak. He made a slipknot in the rope and waited until the contraction ended. The cow made a weak, painful sound.

"That must hurt her." Maggie looked at Tanner with huge, stricken eyes as he slipped the rope in.

"It'll be worse if I can't bring the damned calf around." The next contraction was already upon her, squeezing his arm like a vise. The tiny foot kicked his hand again, hard.

The cow tossed her head, struggling.

Maggie knelt in the snow and grass and mud, stroking the cow's neck. "It's all right, Susie," she crooned softly. "It'll be all right. You'll see."

"Susie?" Tanner's eyes jerked up to meet hers.

Her gaze met his. Her face flushed almost defiantly. "Why not? I don't suppose she has another name?"

He shook his head.

"Then we'll call her Susie. It's more personal that way. Then she'll know we care and that we're trying to help her."

Tanner wasn't sure cows had any idea when you were trying to help them. Sometimes he thought they might. He'd never named one, though. It was hard to name one when you figured it was going to end up on a dinner plate.

"Suit yourself," he muttered. The contraction was lessening. He fumbled with the rope, trying to slip it over the two front feet and bring them around before the next contraction hit.

Getting the feet together was only the beginning of his trouble. Then he had to turn the calf, all the while praying its head would come forward, not lay back.

With each contraction he was forced to wait, to grit his teeth against the fierce pressure on his arm, to hope that he didn't lose the little progress he'd made.

And at each passing he tried to get a grip on the calf's head or shoulder, tried to bring them forward in line with the feet as he pulled on the rope with his other hand.

He was only barely conscious of Maggie. She knelt in the muck, soothing the cow, murmuring to her, with reddened hands rubbing her coarse hide slowly and rhythmically in time with the contractions.

Tanner felt the rope begin to slip and cursed as he lost his grip on the end of it.

"I'll pull."

"You can't . . ."

Maggie pushed a lock of hair out of her face, smudging her cheek with a bit of mud. "She's my cow, isn't she? A fine rancher I'd be if I sat back and let her die."

"All right. Pull slow and steady, just like I was doing, and stop if I tell you."

Maggie nodded. She got to her feet and steadied herself, then started to pull. He could see her new boots, mucky and bloody now, braced in the muddy field just inches from his arm. The next contraction passed. He wriggled his hand behind the calf's neck, applying pressure to bring it in line with the front feet. He felt the movement.

"Yes . . ." The word hissed from between his clenched teeth. His arm trembled. A contraction built once more, the pressure cutting off his circulation again. "Stop!"

Maggie stopped. They waited, motionless, breathing hard, until once more Tanner said, "Now," and started to push slowly and steadily while Maggie pulled.

And this time the calf came free.

The head and forelimbs, along with Tanner's hand, slipped into view. The rest of the calf came quickly after and he caught it, then lay it on the muddy ground.

Maggie dropped the roped and knelt down beside it. "Is it . . ." Her voice was hollow, her face ashen.

Tanner didn't answer. He hunkered down over it and cleared its mouth, then waited. Nothing. He bent and blew into it, forced air down into its lungs once, then again. Again.

It gagged, then choked. All four legs twitched. One eye opened, then the other.

"It's alive!" Maggie exulted. She laughed. She crowed. She crouched down and planted a kiss on its messy head. Then she looked at Tanner, her green eyes sparkling. "You did it! Oh, Robert! You did it!"

And then she launched herself at him and kissed him, too.

The force knocked Tanner flat on his back. His arms came up and went around her all of their own accord. All the breath went right out of him.

The warmth and the weight of her robbed him of whatever coherence the sheer impact hadn't. Only his body responded, and his lips. Hers were warm and wet. His were starving. He couldn't help himself. Desperation could only protect him so far. Common sense simply fled.

When her lips touched his, he kissed her.

It had been years since he'd kissed a woman like that. Fourteen long, hungry, lonely years. There had been women in his life since his divorce from Clare. But they had been few, and none of them had promised more than a night's satisfaction.

Maggie did—as he'd known she would.

The notion terrified him. He jerked his head aside, then grasped her arms and tried to shove her away.

Maggie pulled back, her face flaming. But still she straddled him, and he could feel the press of the juncture of her legs against him. He shoved himself up, but that only made matters worse.

"Oh!" She scrambled off him and he got to his feet, turned his back, adjusted his jeans. "I'm ... sorry," Maggie said in a tiny voice.

"It's all right." It wasn't. It was awful. It had felt so good having her on top of him, her breasts pressing against his chest, her lips on his. He reached over and snagged his hat out of the muck and jammed it on his head.

He hoped to God she hadn't noticed the way his hands had gripped her waist, hadn't felt the instinctive masculine response of his body to her touch.

He got to his knees and ducked his head, reaching for the calf and hauled it up next to the cow's head.

She put out her tongue and gave it a tentative lick. The calf made a noise and nuzzled against her. Her eyes, rheumy and lackluster, brightened. She licked again, nosed her child, licked some more.

"Mother love," Maggie said softly. Her voice sounded just a little bit hoarse.

Tanner nodded. He didn't answer because he knew his would have been a whole lot hoarser. He didn't look at her, either, just gathered up his rope, tugged his hat down harder, then got to his feet and moved toward his horse. Maggie started to follow him, then turned back.

"Look, Robert. Just look at them," Maggie said. "Isn't it wonderful?"

And the joy in her voice brought his gaze around, first to the cow and calf, then, because he couldn't help himself, to her. She was dirty and slightly disheveled, and with just a hint of embarrassment still in her cheeks, she looked positively radiant—the most beautiful woman he'd seen in his entire life, Clare included.

"Wonderful," Tanner croaked, and turned desperately back to his horse.

Four

"**S**he's got a lot of try, that gal," Ev said as he helped Tanner put some new shingles over a leak in the bunk-house roof. He was perched on the ridgepole watching as Maggie learned how to trim hooves from Bates.

Tanner grunted, but he didn't spare her a glance.

"I reckon Abby'd be right proud of the way she's come along."

Tanner kept hammering.

"You'd think she'd have plenty to do, just teaching all them little kids all day. But she's right here pitchin' in every time I turn around. Hell, she's up at dawn fixing break-fast every morning. She's—"

"What d'you mean, she's fixing breakfast? You're dishing up when I come in. She's still upstairs."

"That's 'cause she comes down first, puts on the coffee and makes the pancake batter and gets the bacon goin' while I'm shavin'. Then she goes up and takes a shower and I dish up.''

"She's doin' your job." Tanner scowled.

"I know that. I told her so. She said she likes to."

"Last weekend...the day I took her out with me...did she cook then?''

"Yep. Let me sleep in."

"You shouldn't let her." Tanner was outraged.

Ev grinned. "Tell her that. I tried. She said she's the boss."

Tanner placed a shingle and whacked in a nail with one blow.

He didn't know why it should matter that Maggie was cooking breakfast in the morning. It was still food. What difference did it make who cooked it? Logically, there was no difference at all. Deep down, though, it did matter. It was like she was cooking for him.

He didn't want her doing for him. It made him nervous.

"Reckon she'll want to brand calves next," Ev said with a chuckle. "She and Den Baker were talking yesterday about when the roundup should be."

"That's my job!"

"But it's her ranch," Ev reminded him. "She wasn't making decisions, Tanner. She only wanted to know. Said she was hopin' her brothers would be here. They get off around Easter."

More grief. "The last thing we need is a couple of greenhorns gettin' in the way."

"Maggie ain't getting in the way."

Ain't she? Tanner wanted to ask. He hammered on another shingle.

"Reckon you'd've asked her out by now," Ev said, shooting him a glance out of the corner of his eye.

"Why the hell would I do that?"

"You been vaccinated against pretty women then?"

"She's my boss."

"That don't mean you ain't noticed." Ev grinned slyly. "I reckon she wouldn't care."

"What the hell are you talking about?"

"Her bein' the boss. Reckon she's got an eye for you, too."

"Ouch! Hell!" Tanner popped his hammered thumb into his mouth.

Ev cackled like a crazy man. "Got you goin', don't she? You ain't no steer, Tanner, even if you're tryin' to act like it right now. Maggie's a hell of a fine-lookin' woman, and she likes ranchin'. Just about the best combination there is. So... what're you waitin' for?"

Tanner's hammer hit the roof with a resounding smack. "Mind your own goddamn business!"

Ev just grinned.

"I'm not interested in gettin' tied down," Tanner said in a more modulated tone after a moment. "Not with her. Not with anyone. Besides," he added recklessly, because he knew Ev thought the world of Abby Crumm, "if Ab thought I'd be makin' eyes at her heir, she'd have fired me, not made me promise to stay on."

"You think so, do you?" Ev regarded him over the tops of his spectacles. "Well, she wasn't no fool, our Ab. But just go right on foolin' yourself if you want."

Tanner snorted, not dignifying that remark with a reply. Any answer he made would play right into whatever trap Ev was laying next.

But Ev didn't say anything else, just began to whistle softly, looking up every once in a while to watch Maggie as she bent over the horse's hoof.

Tanner watched, too. He couldn't help it. There was something about a trim female in jeans that caught a man's attention. Bates didn't have to bend so damned close to her, for God's sake. He was practically hugging her!

Tanner shifted irritably, adjusting his jeans, and, with his heel, knocked the hammer to the ground.

"Hell!"

Ev laughed at him.

It wasn't funny. Not a bit. He didn't want this, didn't want the temptation, the distraction that Maggie brought into his life. But even when he tried to avoid her, it didn't work. She was everywhere he went.

Like Ev, he'd assumed that a full-time teaching job would leave her little time to intrude in his life.

He hadn't counted on riding in one afternoon to find Maggie and four third graders crouched in a stall in the barn. "What the hell—I mean, heck—are you doing?"

Maggie looked up and smiled at him. Even now, every time she did it, it felt like a kick in the gut. "Would you believe that some of my children have never seen a cow up close, even in Wyoming? I wanted to show them Grace."

Tanner stifled a groan. Grace—God help him—was a calf. An orphan calf he'd found bawling next to its dead mother in last Sunday's snowstorm. He tried to get another mother cow to take it, but none had lost a calf and he didn't have a prayer. So he'd brought it in slung over the front of the saddle.

Maggie had taken it over—and named it Grace.

"Because it was through the grace of God that you found her and brought her home," she told Tanner quite seriously, her wide green eyes luminous as she'd looked up at him from where she knelt on the floor of the barn, feeding the calf.

She was looking like an angel again. "Suit yourself," he muttered, beating a hasty retreat.

It seemed like every time he went into the barn after that, Maggie was there feeding Grace. And now she had a circle of eight-year-olds sitting there with her, with Billy showing them the bucket with the nipple, demonstrating how the feeding was done. Ev was always telling him that Billy's teachers couldn't get a word out of him. They should see him now, Tanner thought.

He was unsaddling Gambler when Maggie appeared at his side. He stepped back, her nearness still capable of unnerving him.

"Grace is a big hit." She smiled at him, then looked over to where Billy was helping one of the girls give Grace the bottle. "They love her."

"They don't have to feed her day and night."

"My, aren't you grumpy this afternoon," she teased. "Get up on the wrong side of bed?"

"Lucky when I can get to bed." For the last four nights he'd been out with calving cows.

"Should we hire someone to help you?"

"Waste of money. I can do it myself. Anyway, looks like no one's ready to calve tonight, so I'll have a break."

"Good. You can take the children back to Casper with me."

"*What*? I can't do that!"

"Why not? I'd like the chance to sit down and talk to you uninterrupted."

"No, I—"

"We haven't really had a chance since I moved in. You've been busy and so have I. But tonight—"

"I can't!" Tanner said desperately. "I've got to—got to—to muck out the barn."

"I'll help you muck out the barn when we come back."

"No!"

Maggie cocked her head. "You know, Robert," she said, one corner of her mouth lifting as she looked straight at him, "the way you're constantly trying to avoid me, I could get the impression that you're afraid of me."

"I am not afraid of you!"

"Really? Then prove it."

He ought to know better than to take a dare. Damn it, his brother Luke was the one who took dares, not him.

But what was he supposed to do when Maggie lifted her chin and grinned knowingly at him like that? He sure as hell wasn't going to let her think he was running scared.

Probably it was a good thing, he told himself, being forced. Maybe what he needed was a few hours of non-stop company with Maggie MacLeod. Maybe then whatever itch she was inspiring in him would be scratched. In any case, he didn't see that he had much choice.

They took the utility truck, which had plenty of room for all the kids when he put the seat back in. It also gave him plenty of elbow room in the front seat—as long as Maggie didn't do anything stupid like slide over and sit next to him.

The moment the thought occurred to him, he glanced in her direction. But she was turned and talking to the children in the back, asking them what they thought about feeding Grace, and he began to relax a little.

He liked listening to her talk to the kids. She wasn't patronizing like a lot of his teachers had been. And she didn't bark out orders to them, either. She seemed genuinely interested in them. And they were equally interested in her. They knew all about her life, it seemed to Tanner. About her parents and her brothers and the places she'd lived growing up.

"Do you like it better here or in the jungle?" one of the little boys asked her.

"Oh, here," Maggie said. "But the jungle was interesting. You should go sometime."

The boy's eyes widened. "You really think I could?"

"If you want to bad enough," Maggie told him.

"Like you wanted your home?" one of the girls asked her.

"Just like that, Dena," Maggie said. "I was extremely blessed by Miss Crumm's generosity, of course. But I would have made a home wherever I settled. She just made it possible for me to be here."

"How long you gonna stay?" the boy asked.

"For the rest of my life, I hope."

"You stayin', too, Mr. Tanner?" he asked.

"Not me," Tanner said.

"How come?" The boy bounced forward on the seat to peer over into Tanner's face. "Don'tcha like Miz Mac-Leod?"

"Sure I like her," Tanner said, flexing his fingers on the steering wheel. The truck seemed suddenly to be getting smaller.

"Then how come you're gonna leave?"

"Because it's what *I* want to do." Need to do, his mind raged silently.

"You know what I think?" Dena said. "I think you should marry her."

Tanner's head whipped around so fast he almost drove right off the road. Maggie pressed her fist to her mouth to stop a smile, then turned to Dena and said gently, "I think that's a decision best left up to Mr. Tanner and me, Dena."

The girl kicked her foot against the back of the seat in front of her. "I was only sayin'. Don't you want to get married?"

"Yes," Maggie said.

"No," said Tanner.

Maggie looked at him for a second before turning back to Dena. "There. You see?" she said lightly. "It would never work. Come on now, look where the sun is setting. Who can tell me what direction we're going?"

She kept them talking until they were all dropped off and she and Tanner were sitting alone in the truck together.

"Sorry about that," she said, folding her hands in her lap. "I didn't imagine they were going to try their hand at matchmaking."

He shrugged. "Doesn't matter." He hoped she didn't notice the high line of color that he was sure still tinged his cheekbones. He put the truck in gear. "You need to do some shopping before we head back?"

"A little," Maggie said. "And then I'm taking you to dinner."

He protested. She pulled rank. He grumbled.

She laughed. "I think I'm beginning to like this 'boss' business. Come on into the grocery store with me."

He didn't argue this time. He didn't remember much Shakespeare from high school, but he did remember the bit about protesting too much. Besides, he didn't see what harm he could come to with her in the grocery store. Which just went to show how shortsighted he was.

It was like being married to her. Maybe it was just that he had marriage on the brain after what Dena had said. But he couldn't help it.

Married people went grocery shopping together.

He remembered doing it with Clare—walking down the aisles side by side, him pushing the cart, her picking things off the shelves, looking to him now and then for approval. Maggie did it now, seeking wordless approval for some package of beans and rice she was considering. It tore at his gut.

He shoved the cart at her. "Think I'll just get some air," he said, and headed rapidly for the exit.

He was pacing around outside, feeling like an idiot, when Maggie came out ten minutes later and apologized to him. "Sorry about taking so long. But I'll make it up to you. I know a great place to go for dinner."

Once more he tried to convince her they didn't need to go out to dinner. Once more she won.

"We need to talk. If we're going to work together, we need to get to know each other."

Tanner thought he knew her better than he wanted to already, but he couldn't tell her that. "So, fine. Let's go. Got any ideas?"

She did. Her choice surprised him. She directed him back out of Casper and north on the highway to Kaycee. "It's fabulous. They have the best smothered green chile burritos in the world," she told him.

"I know."

His response made her blink, then laugh. "Of course you do. Why do I think I'm the first one to discover these places?"

In fact, he'd eaten there plenty of times. And Maggie was right: they did have the best smothered green chile burritos he'd ever eaten. But somehow tonight they tasted even better.

It was because of Maggie. Tanner knew it. He knew, too, that he shouldn't enjoy it, that it was dangerous as hell to let down his guard with her even for an evening. But he couldn't seem to help it. Her enthusiasm made him smile in spite of himself. Everybody knew her. Everybody greeted her with a comment and a grin. They grinned at him, too.

"Got yourself a looker, eh, Tanner?" one of the waitresses said to him.

He opened his mouth to deny it, then couldn't. After all, it was true. He shrugged, glancing down at Maggie by his side. Just for the moment, why not just go along for the ride? It was a little like the way his brother described bronc riding. "If I can't control it, hey, I just try to hang in there and enjoy the trip," Noah had said with a grin. "Sometimes that's enough to keep me from getting my butt kicked."

Tanner prayed that the same would apply to a dinner with Maggie. He looked at her as the waitress left after taking their order.

"You come here a lot?"

"One of the waitresses is the mother of one of my kids. She can't make it to conferences very often because she has so far to drive, so I stop in on my way home and she feeds me and we talk." Her brow wrinkled. "You don't think that's a conflict of interest, do you?"

"I don't know," Tanner said, deadpan. "Depends on if the kid's grades are improving."

Maggie laughed. "I only wish they were." She sipped at the beer the waitress set in front of her. "Were you a good student, Robert?"

"Tanner," he corrected. "No, I wasn't."

"Me, neither. We moved around too much. And then, when I had to come back to the States for high school, I missed my parents and brothers dreadfully. I wrote letters all the time. I never studied."

That surprised him. He'd had her pegged for a straight-A student, a Little Miss Perfect, and he'd never imagined her lonely. He didn't like to think about her needing someone and not having them. "You must've done all right," he said after a moment. "You're a teacher now."

"Because I worked hard and because I wanted to be."

"You're lucky to have gone to college."

"You didn't?"

"No." He wasn't going to say anything else, but she didn't comment, just looked at him expectantly, so he went on. "It wasn't that I wouldn't have liked to. There wasn't enough money when I got out of high school. I was saving what I could out of the little I made, thought maybe I'd go the next year. But then my father died."

"And he didn't leave you any legacy?"

"Oh yeah, there was a legacy. He left me my brothers. They were seventeen and fifteen."

Maggie whistled under her breath. "It must have been so hard on you. How did you manage?"

"Badly." And he didn't care how long she waited, he wasn't expanding on that.

Maggie smiled. "I doubt that. You strike me as a very capable man. Very responsible."

"I tried," Tanner muttered. She didn't have to know how he'd failed.

"What are they doing now?"

"Luke—he's the older one—is in California. He's the stunt double for Keith Mallory."

"Keith Mallory?" Maggie's eyes bugged at the mention of one of Hollywood's most popular young actors.

"Luke got all the looks," Tanner said wryly, "and none of the common sense. You know the sort of pictures Mallory does?"

Maggie nodded. They were almost all action-and-reaction, bar-fights-and-bedlam, horse-and-car-chase flicks.

"Well, he and Luke are a match made in heaven 'cause Luke never met a stunt he wouldn't try."

The job, which had come by the fluke of Lucas's simply being in the right place at the right time, had been his brother's salvation, as far as Tanner could see. Doing most of Keith's stunts had provided a channel for his recklessness, a positive use for energy that all too often threatened to spin out of control.

The waitress brought their burritos and two glasses of beer. Maggie took a bite before asking, "What about the other one? I suppose he's a rocket scientist."

"Noah? Hardly. He's a rodeo bronc rider. A damned good one. He's gone to the NFR the last five years in a row."

"NFR?"

"National Finals Rodeo. They have it every December in Vegas. Only the top fifteen money winners in each event get to go. Like I said, he's good."

"You must be very proud of both of them."

"They turned out okay, I guess." There was no need to tell her that it had been far from smooth sailing for any of them.

"Will I get to meet them?"

"I don't see much of 'em, but they call sometimes. Feel sorry for me stuck out in the back of the beyond, I guess." He gave an awkward shrug and bent his head, concentrating on his burrito again. He wasn't used to talking this much. Maybe it was the beer. Or maybe it was just that Maggie was easy to talk to. *Too* easy to talk to.

He changed the subject. "What about your brothers?"

So she told him about her brothers—about Duncan, the elder, who was working on an advanced degree in geography at the University of Colorado, and about Andy, who was an undergraduate at Wyoming.

"He doesn't know what he wants to do," she told Tanner finally, after having described a few of Andy's more daring scrapes. "He's at loose ends academically. I think he'll like the ranch. He keeps telling me he wants to be a cowboy."

Tanner drained his beer. "A right-thinking man."

"I'm sure he'll be delighted when you tell him so. He's coming this weekend."

Tanner had forgotten that. It was a measure of how much he was mellowing under the influence of good food and beer that he didn't feel his customary protest welling up inside. He finished his burrito and pushed his plate away. The waitress poured him some coffee and he lifted the cup to his mouth, settling back in the booth and sipping it.

Surely it wouldn't hurt just to look at her. He wasn't buying; he knew that. But just this once, for a few stolen moments...

Maggie looked up and saw him watching her. "Are you in a hurry?"

He shook his head. "Tell me about this jungle you grew up in."

She did, talking easily and with fondness about her growing-up years. Listening to her, Tanner could imagine her as a child, all knobby knees and eager grins, and then as a teenager coming to the States, her enthusiasm more cautious, her eyes more wary. He could see all those things and more in the woman she'd become.

Maggie took a swallow of coffee. "I'm talking too much."

"No." He could have listened all night.

"But we have the barn to muck out, remember?" She grinned at him.

"Forget the barn. I'll get Bates to help in the morning."

"Well, we probably ought to go anyway. We have to get up early."

He knew she didn't mean it the way he took it. He knew it was only his imagination that had them getting up together. The waitress brought their bill. Maggie reached for it. Tanner got it first.

"I invited you," Maggie protested.

"Tough." It was like looking at her for just a moment had been—wishing. Indulging himself in just the smallest bit of pretence, the fantasy that he'd really had a date with Maggie MacLeod.

Of course, he knew he hadn't. But damn it, if a guy couldn't have reality, if he had to make do with dreams, was it such a crime if he based those dreams on what little he could muster from real life?

It was dark as they walked to the truck. The wind was cold and there was still frost in the air, and if he'd dared, he'd have slipped his arm around her as they walked. He did open the door for her. Another little bit of fantasy. She thanked him. Her voice was soft. He almost had to strain to hear it. He got in the driver's side and started up the engine. For just a moment he wished she'd slide over next to him, let her hip press against his.

But there was only so much reality that a fantasy could stand. That would be carrying things too far.

He flicked on the radio as they drove. Neither of them spoke. Just as well. Anything they said would spoil it, tip the balance, kill his dream.

He wasn't so dreamy that he forgot to do his job. He stopped to check on the cattle on the way to the house. "You can drive home if you want," he said as he got out of the truck. "It's not that far. I can walk."

"I'll wait," Maggie said, and she smiled at him in the moonlight. His heart kicked over.

Careful, he warned himself. *It isn't going to happen.*

It couldn't happen. He wouldn't let it.

He only wanted the dream. The cattle cooperated. He was back in the truck within twenty minutes. "All's well," he said, rubbing his hands together, then started up the engine.

He helped her carry the groceries into the house. There were only two bags. She could have managed alone, but he couldn't seem to let go. After they'd put the groceries away and he'd asked for and received a glass of water, he had no other choice.

He slanted her a smile and backed toward the door. "I'll, er, see you tomorrow."

Maggie followed him onto the porch. "Yes. Thank you for dinner. I didn't intend for you to pay for it."

"I wanted to."

They looked at each other for a long moment. He wanted to kiss her. He remembered the time she'd kissed him, when their lips had touched, when his body had burned. Maggie ran her tongue over her lips. He shut his eyes.

He knew his limits. Kissing her was beyond them. He hurried down the steps.

"Robert?"

He glared at her. She grinned. "I just wanted to say how much I enjoyed the evening, the company."

"Me, too," he said, then strode quickly across the yard. It was no more than the truth. He had enjoyed it. Far too much.

Five

Maggie's brothers showed up exactly as predicted, the week before Easter. Duncan, the elder, was tall and dark-haired and serious. "The Professor," Ev called him, half teasing, half respectful. He called the younger brother, Andy, "The Pest." Tanner called him "City Slicker" or "Slicker" for short. Andy didn't mind.

A freckle-faced, bright-eyed redhead who was even more irrepressible than his sister, Andy MacLeod wanted to do everything, see everything, learn everything at once. And most of all he wanted to emulate Tanner.

Somehow or other—whether from Maggie or Ev, Tanner never knew—Andy had determined that he was the font of all ranching knowledge. He followed him like a puppy.

At first Tanner grumbled about it. "It isn't like I don't have enough to do," he complained to Ev. "Now I've got a shadow wherever I go."

But Andy's willingness to admit ignorance and his determination to learn the ropes won even Tanner's grudging admiration before long.

He was a better rider than his sister and an instinctively good roper. He even did dirty work like digging postholes, but what cemented him in Tanner's high regard was that he didn't bat an eye when Tanner suggested that he muck out the barn.

"It's part of the job, isn't it?" Andy said.

"Bates doesn't seem to think so."

Andy grinned. "My dad always says that if you're going to run things you've got to know how to do everything from the ground up."

"You planning on running things, are you, Slicker?"

Andy colored fiercely. "I didn't mean that," he said quickly. "I'm not after your job, Tanner. I swear I'm not."

"It's okay," he said easily. "I know that."

In spite of himself, he liked Andy. If he told Andy to try something, Andy tried it. "You got to learn by doing," Tanner told him, the way Tanner's father had taught him in turn. So Andy did. The boy's persistence impressed him. Although he supposed he shouldn't have been surprised. Not after Maggie.

Maggie.

Always there was Maggie. It had been a mistake going out with her. It had been hard enough to control his attraction before he'd fed his fantasies. Now he was a wreck. He daydreamed constantly. His nights were worse. He had a prayer of controlling his thoughts during the daylight hours. At night he was at the mercy of his desires. And his desire was for Maggie. It didn't matter that he told himself she was off-limits, that she wasn't a one-night-stand woman, that she'd want forever while he wanted anything but.

It didn't matter because wherever he went, there she was. She had a week's vacation for spring break while her brothers were home and she spent it with them. And that meant she spent it with him.

Oh, every once in a while she would stay in the house and go over some book work with Duncan. But mostly she rode out with Andy—and Tanner.

"You don't need to," Tanner told her time and again. "That's what you have a foreman for."

"I need to," Maggie said. "I want to."

There was no arguing with her.

So he'd hoped to get a little respite in the evenings when he could retreat to the bunkhouse. He reckoned without Andy.

"Why sit down there by yourself," Andy asked him, "when you can be up here with us? Maggie and I are makin' doughnuts tonight. Why don't you come?"

Reluctantly, Tanner came. Maggie tied an apron around his waist and set him to work mixing flour and baking powder and stuff.

"Might've known you'd put me to work," he complained. But he had a good time.

The next night Andy followed him back down to the bunkhouse after supper and kept talking to him, assuming that Tanner would be coming up with him when he returned. Tanner couldn't think of a good reason not to, so he went. It had begun to sleet and there was a cold wind coming down out of the mountains.

Duncan had laid a fire in the fireplace, and a Bob Marley CD played on Maggie's stereo. Ev was teaching Billy and Duncan how to play cribbage. Maggie was sitting on the sofa with one of the scrapbooks of the history of the ranch that Abigail had left.

"Show me," Andy commanded, and Maggie made room for him on the couch.

"Come join us," she invited Tanner.

He shook his head. "I'm fine right here."

He sat in the old wing chair stretching out his sock-clad feet in front of the fire, listened to the patter of sleet against the window and watched them all.

It was the sort of evening he'd once dreamed about having when he was married to Clare—the sort he remembered from when he was a very little boy.

Only instead of Ev bent over the dining room table, his bald head between Duncan's dark and Billy's fair one, Tanner remembered days when his father had taught him and his brothers how to play cribbage. He listened to Andy and Maggie murmur and laugh over the scrapbooks and remembered when he and Luke used to go through the Christmas scrapbooks their mother had made for them. He wondered for the first time in ages what had become of them.

Thinking about his mother, remembering her and the warmth of his childhood years, made him restless. He got to his feet and wandered toward the window.

"Bored?" Maggie materialized at his elbow while he was staring out into the darkness, still feeling that indefinable longing.

He looked at her, felt another kind of longing, shook his head quickly and moved away.

Maggie frowned. "How about joining Andy and me for a game of Scrabble?"

"I'm not much for games," Tanner said gruffly, and then cursed himself silently when she looked even more unhappy.

He didn't want her to think he didn't like her, didn't like being invited to join them. He did like it! He liked it too damned much! If she knew the way he really felt about being around her... If she knew the sorts of dreams he had, both awake and sleeping...

He rubbed the back of his neck, the combined tension and arousal he always felt around her getting worse, not better. "I ought to check the cattle one more time anyhow, then turn in. Gotta roll out early."

"We'll go with you."

"No!"

She looked at him, startled, her frown deepening further.

"I mean—" he moderated his tone "—there's no use you coming. I'll be fine on my own. Besides—" he said, giving her a faint grin, "—only fools or cowboys voluntarily go out in weather like this."

Maggie smiled gently. "Maybe I'm a fool—" she began, and at the look in her eyes, Tanner quailed.

He shook his head abruptly. "You're not."

And he was out the door and down the steps before she could follow him. He didn't look back until he was almost to the barn. She was still standing in the door, watching him.

He noticed the strange truck the minute he rode into the yard. He thought he knew most of the trucks within fifty miles. There weren't that many. But he didn't know anyone with a new Dodge 250 with an extended cab. He rode past it slowly, allowing his curiosity to dictate Gambler's pace. It had Wyoming plates starting with a 5. Laramie or thereabouts. He frowned, wondering who they knew from Laramie.

"Whose truck?" he asked Billy when the boy appeared on the porch.

"His name's John," Billy said.

"John who?"

"Dunno. He's a friend of Maggie's."

Tanner took off his hat and shoved his fingers through his hair, then continued on his way to the barn, shooting one last glance over his shoulder toward the house, curious about this friend of Maggie's. He told himself he shouldn't be. It was none of his business who her friends were.

Andy was in the barn when he led Gambler to his stall. Tanner was surprised to see him.

"You're in early."

"I ran into Maggie and John up near Teller's Point. They helped me finish checking the fence and I came down with them."

Tanner frowned, not at all sure he wanted anybody else checking the fences. But then, it was Maggie's ranch. If she wanted to do it, it shouldn't matter to him. "Who's John?" he asked Andy.

"Haven't you met him yet? I know Maggie wants you to. He's a friend of hers from college. Now he's getting his Ph.D. in agricultural economics or something at UW. Sharp guy. You'll like him."

Tanner grunted. He unsaddled Gambler. Andy finished with his horse. "I did Sunny and Randy, too," he told Tanner. "Maggie and John rode 'em up on the range. But I told Maggie I'd brush 'em down so she'd have time to show John the books."

Tanner's brows drew down as he bent over Gambler's hoof with the pick. What the hell was she showing John the books for? The Three Bar C's finances weren't any business of his. Tanner flipped extra hard at a piece of hardened mud, hit the frog and got kicked for his trouble.

"Damn! Sorry," he muttered to the horse. Gambler edged sideways uneasily. Tanner murmured soothingly, trying to concentrate on what he was doing.

"Well, I'm off!" Andy said cheerfully. "I'll see you in the house for supper." He paused at the door to the barn. "Sure will miss this place."

Tanner looked up. "When're you leaving?" Their holiday was almost over. Duncan had left last night for Boulder.

"I'm riding back with John tonight."

"Oh. Good."

"Good?" Andy yelped.

"I didn't mean that. I meant…" But he could hardly say he felt unaccountably relieved at this reason for the mysterious John's arrival. "I just meant it's good you've got a ride. And you'll be back before you know it."

"Four weeks," Andy said. "Not quite actually. Twenty-seven days till my last final's over." He grinned sheepishly. "I counted. Promise you won't have the roundup till I get here."

"Well…" Tanner drew the word out, enjoying the look of dismay growing on Andy's face by the second. "No, Slicker, we'll wait for you."

Andy grinned. "Thanks, Tanner. See you at supper."

They were eating in the dining room. They ate in the dining room at Thanksgiving, Christmas and Easter. They were using Ab's good family china, the stuff her grandmother had brought out from Maryland in a covered wagon or some damned thing. Tanner wondered if he should've worn a suit and said so.

"Don't be ridiculous," Maggie laughed. She reached out and took his hand, drawing him toward the living room. "Come and meet John. He's a very old and dear friend of mine."

Tanner allowed himself to be towed. In the living room, sitting in the wing chair, was a lean, bespectacled, dark-haired man dressed in jeans and a sweater. He had the sort of features that had never been rearranged by a bronc. Women probably liked him. A lot. Tanner figured he was in his late twenties. He had one of the ranch ledgers on his lap, but he set it aside and stood up when Maggie came in.

"John, this is my foreman and the man who keeps things going around here, Robert Tanner. Robert, this is John Merritt. We went to boarding school out east together, then we went to college together. For years John was all the family I had. He's in Laramie now working on his doctorate. Land use and reform is his specialty, so I've been talking to him about the Three Bar C."

John Merritt held out his hand, smiling and studying Tanner with about as much curiosity as Tanner felt about him. "Pleased to meet you, Robert. Or do you prefer Bob?"

"Tanner," Tanner said through his teeth. "Everyone calls me Tanner."

Merritt grinned. "Except Maggie." He gave her a fond look and tugged at her hair, which she had pulled back in a leather thong against the nape of her neck. "I know Maggie. She's a law unto herself, isn't she?"

Tanner felt his jaw tighten at the familiarity between them. He had to consciously will himself to relax before he nodded his head.

"Do you want something to drink before dinner?" Maggie asked him. "Ev says it will be another fifteen minutes or so before it's ready."

Tanner hesitated, noticed the glass of wine by the chair where John had been sitting and shrugged. "I'll have a whiskey."

Maggie looked momentarily taken aback, then she smiled. "Of course. Ev, where's the—" she raised her voice to call.

But Tanner cut in. "I'll get it."

It was another gut feeling that Bates could have put a name to—probably something to do with a deep-seated male need to defend his territory. Tanner didn't care what anyone called it as long as John Merritt acknowledged that he was the trespasser at the Three Bar C, that this was Tanner's domain, not his.

He strode over to the buffet and opened the door, took out the bottle of whiskey that he and Ev and Abby had last opened when they'd toasted the New Year, and poured himself a generous dollop, then added a bit more for good measure. He turned, his eyes flicking over Maggie, John, Ev, Billy and Andy who were all looking at him.

"Want any?"

Ev, Maggie and John declined.

"I might—" Andy began. But Maggie said, "Don't even think it." And when John added, "Not if you plan on doing any driving tonight," Andy subsided with a rueful shrug.

"I'll have one for you," Tanner told him, swallowing the liquid in one fiery gulp, then pouring himself another.

"I reckon it's just about time we ate," Ev said hurriedly. "Come on, young man," he said, chivying Billy ahead of him toward the kitchen. "You can help me bring out the food. You might want to lend me a hand, too," he said to Tanner, giving him an arch look.

Tanner followed him into the kitchen. "What do you need me for?"

Ev snorted and muttered something that sounded very much like "I don't," before he thrust the handle of a carving knife at Tanner and said, "Carve the roast, while I make the gravy."

"Why me?"

"Because if you're going to do any carving, I'd just as soon it was on the meat and not the company." He handed Billy the bowl of mashed potatoes and steered him toward the dining room.

"What the hell's that supposed to mean?" Tanner demanded.

"It means settle down. It means stop knockin' back the whiskey like the state's goin' dry tomorrow. It means stop bristlin' like a mad dog about to attack."

"I wasn't going to attack," Tanner protested.

"Coulda fooled me," Ev muttered. "Carve the roast."

Tanner carved. It was just that sometimes you met a guy who set your teeth on edge. Nothing personal. Just bad vibes. He couldn't help it. It was like that with him and Merritt from the moment he'd laid eyes on the other man.

He made quick work of the roast, more aware of the muted sounds in the living room—of Andy's eager voice, Maggie's soft tones and Merritt's deeper, scholarly ones— than of the meat he was cutting.

"Hell, you don't have to cut it in bite-sized pieces," Ev grumbled. "G'wan in to supper." He paused. "And behave yourself."

Muttering under his breath, Tanner went. He sat. He dished food onto his plate. He ate with stolid determination. He didn't say a word. He listened while John and Maggie reminisced about their boarding-school days. About the time John had done something dreadful to a hated Latin teacher, and about the time Maggie had done something even worse, the details of which were lost in gales of laughter that set Tanner's teeth on edge. He listened while Andy told John all the things he'd learned about cowboying during his week at the ranch, and listened with increasing irritation while John encouraged him.

"There's a lot to learn, isn't there, Tanner?" he said, lifting his gaze to meet Tanner's.

"Mmph," Tanner said through a mouthful of mashed potatoes.

"It's good to learn from someone who can give you hands-on experience," John went on. "You're lucky," he told Andy.

"I know it," Andy said. "Tanner's the best."

"He certainly seems to be doing the best with what's here," John said. "I told Maggie that when she took me out to see the ranch today." He and Maggie shared a smile.

Tanner stabbed a piece of roast with considerable force.

"But it's hard to make a ranch break even these days," John went on. "Unless you diversify."

Tanner stopped chewing. His eyes narrowed.

Encouraged by what must have appeared to be avid interest, Merritt went on. "There is a place, though, near—what's it called? Teller's Point—that is a little too steep for cattle. To make the best use of the land there, I was telling Maggie she ought to consider sheep."

"Sheep?" Tanner's fork hit the plate with a clatter. His fists clenched. He stared bug-eyed at the man across the table from him.

John laughed. "I know, I know. The old animosities die hard. But it's prime sheep land, Tanner. Rockier than the rest of your range. Not as good grass. Sheep can handle it. Cattle can't. I know Miss Crumm's ancestors are most probably spinning in their graves at the very notion of sheep at the Three Bar C, but Maggie agrees that—"

Maggie agrees?

"Ab's ancestors be damned! *I'm* spinnin' right here," Tanner came close to yelling. "Sheep!" He fairly spat the word. He fixed a glare on Maggie. "What the hell are you doing, bringing some highfalutin' expert in? Don't you think I know a damned thing? I may not have the book-learning he does, but I've been around a damned sight longer. But I forgot, this is your *home* now, isn't it? You can do what you want! Well, fine, do it. I'll bet Ab's real pleased!"

He tossed his napkin on his plate, shoved back his chair, stood up. He almost broke a pane of glass in the door when he slammed it on his way out.

"Well, it's about time."

Tanner stopped dead on the steps of the bunkhouse as Maggie's voice came to him out of the darkness.

"What do you want?" He tried to make out where she was.

Then he heard the chair squeak on the narrow porch and saw a dark form rise. He took a deep breath and brushed past her, opening the door and flicking on the light.

"To talk to you," Maggie said, following him in.

"Hope you haven't been waiting long...Boss." He shed his jacket and tossed his hat onto the dresser, only then glancing over his shoulder.

She was wearing the slacks and angora sweater she'd worn the first time he'd seen her. Her cheeks were red and he wondered guiltily how long she'd been sitting out there, then told himself that it was her problem if she wanted to lurk around in the cold waiting for him. He was just doing his job.

Tanner kicked out a chair. "Talk away."

She sat. He stayed standing with his elbows braced against the wall behind him.

"You were rude tonight."

He shifted uncomfortably. "So?"

"I was embarrassed."

"I'm not your kid! You don't have to be embarrassed on account of me."

"I do if you act like a jerk in my house."

He scuffed the toe of his boot on the plank floor. "Sorry." His tone was truculent. He couldn't help it. It had been five hours and he was still mad. Bad enough she had to drag home her smart friends, but when they started telling him how to run the ranch—!

"I'm sorry, too," Maggie said quietly. "I wasn't trying to undermine your authority tonight. And John didn't mean to imply that you didn't know what you were doing."

"No kiddin'?" Tanner said with just a hint of sarcasm. He breathed a little more easily. At least she thought his reaction had to do with the sheep. He strode over to the window and stared out into the blackness.

"No, he didn't," Maggie said firmly. "And you know it, too."

"I do? How?"

"Because you suggested sheep to Abby yourself!"

Tanner's head whipped around and he stared at her. "How the hell do you know?"

"Because Ev told me."

Tanner cursed under his breath. He clenched his fists.

"He told me it was a long-standing battle between you and Abby," Maggie went on implacably. "He said you used to argue about it daily."

"I mighta mentioned it once or twice," Tanner said to the wall. "I'm no damned *agricultural economist*," he gave the words a bitter twist, "so you can imagine how much attention Ab paid to what I said."

It was Maggie's turn to say a rude word. Tanner looked at her, shocked.

"If you can swear, so can I." She stood up abruptly and faced him head-on. "So what I want to know is, if you weren't mad about the sheep, just exactly why did you slam out of the house?"

Tanner jammed his hands into the pockets of his jeans. "Never mind." He stared away from her resolutely.

She reached for his arm and tried to turn him to face her. Her touch scorched him. He jumped as if he were burned, looked for an escape, but he was backed into a corner. Maggie stood between him and the door.

"No, I want to mind. I want to talk about it. And I want to know why it is that every time I come near you, you run off like some spooked stallion."

Because that was exactly what he felt like! "If it bothers you, stop comin' near me," Tanner snapped, still trying to edge away.

Maggie didn't move. "It is sexual." She said the words in wonderment, as if the revelation had just dawned on her.

"What the hell's that supposed to mean? What's sexual?" He felt as if his face was on fire. He almost couldn't say the word in front of her.

"Why you're running." Her expression changed. A smile replaced the wonderment.

"I'm not running!"

Maggie shook her head, still smiling, looking at him. "Yes," she said softly, "You are."

Hell. He gritted his teeth and looked away.

Suddenly her expression grew serious. "Don't you...like women, Robert?"

His gaze whipped back to meet hers. "Damn! Of course I like women!" The tips of his ears were burning.

Maggie's smile returned. She sighed with obvious relief. "Well, I'm glad to hear it." Then she sobered. "So is it me?"

"Is what you?" He felt as if he were strangling.

"Do you think I'm going to attack you?"

God, didn't he wish! "No, damn it, of course I don't think you're going to attack me!"

"Perhaps you're afraid of sexual harassment."

"What?"

"Well, I am your employer. And it just occurred to me that you might be afraid of us having more than, um, a working relationship... that I might start to expect you to..." For the first time, Maggie faltered. Her cheeks reddened.

Tanner drew his tongue across his upper lip, unsure whether or not to be glad she seemed to be getting as flustered as he was. "I don't think you're going to jump my bones," he said gruffly.

"I won't," Maggie promised solemnly. Then she cocked her head. "But not because I haven't been tempted."

Tanner's eyes widened. He hadn't thought it was possible to feel any more uncomfortable. He was wrong. He swallowed. Hard. He scowled at her, expecting her to blush and look away.

But she was looking at him with frank appreciation and he was the one who ended up with the blush suffusing his face.

"Don't be ridiculous," he muttered, turning away from her.

"I'm not. You're a very handsome man. A strong man. A capable man. I'd have to be blind not to be attracted."

"You're not attracted," Tanner said hoarsely.

"Do you think if you keep telling yourself that, it will be true?"

"It better be true."

"Why?"

"Because," Tanner muttered. "Just because." God, why was she doing this to him? Did she enjoy watching him squirm?

"Because you're attracted, too?" He heard her move, heard her footsteps approach on the smooth plank floor. And then she was so close he could swear he felt her breath against his back.

He wheeled around to face her, breathing fire. "I am not attracted to you!"

Their gazes met, locked. They stood frozen in time for so long that Tanner thought they might stay that way forever.

Finally Maggie spoke. "Ah, Robert," she said softly. "Ab said it, but I didn't believe it."

"What are you talking about?" he rasped.

"She said you were always trying not to care. She said that you didn't want to. She said someday she hoped you'd stop lying to yourself."

"I've had enough of your meddling," Tanner told Abby. He stood, bareheaded, and kicked at the fresh-mown grass in the little hillside cemetery where lay the last earthly remains of Abigail Crumm. He was glad there was no one else around to hear him.

He felt sure Abby did.

"First you sic this city-slicker girl on me. Then you start tellin' her how I think. Hell, woman, when'd you ever know how I thought?" He paused, recollecting. "Well, besides the times you knew I was looking for a fight and you wouldn't let me find one." He scuffed his toe in the grass again.

"This isn't like that. This is different. You got no business meddlin' here. You had no business makin' me promise to stay. None."

He stared hard at her headstone, as if it might channel some sort of response.

"It was like you were matchmaking." He fixed the headstone with a hard glare. "Were you?"

This time he didn't need an answer. He could see Ab's enigmatic smile in his mind's eye, could see the teasing glint she'd have had in her pale green ones.

He shrugged. "It's part my fault, I suppose. You didn't know. I should've told you . . . about . . . about Clare. But you know now. I'm sure you know now. If you got to heaven, Ab, damn it, you've got to know! So you got to know it won't work!" He looked at the headstone pleadingly.

He sighed and bent his head. "Anyway, I can't do it any longer. I can't."

If he'd expected a voice from on high to liberate him from his promise, he was waiting in vain.

And even as he said the words, he saw Ab the way she'd been the day he'd made the promise. It had been only two days before her death. She was getting progressively weaker, but Tanner hadn't wanted to admit it at the time. Abby had known the truth. She, unlike Tanner, had never lied to herself.

"So, you're a better man than I am, Abby Crumm," Tanner said hoarsely now.

But even admitting it, he knew he owed her.

She'd given him a chance to show what he knew, to take all those years of working for some other boss and prove what he'd learned. She'd even given him the chance to own his own ranch, but he'd been afraid to take it. She hadn't reproached him. She'd been quiet, but gentle. She'd understood.

And now he was standing here trying to break the one promise he'd made to her.

Why?

Because he was afraid. Afraid of his own emotions. Afraid of getting too close to Maggie MacLeod.

If he fell in love with Maggie, he'd want to marry her. And he didn't want to fail again. Not the way he'd failed Clare.

So go, he told himself. Maggie would let him leave. She wouldn't hold him to the promise he'd made Abby. She'd find someone else to run the Three Bar C until Andy was ready for the job.

Hell, she could probably ask Merritt to find her the best man in Wyoming.

And did he want that? Tanner asked himself.

He rubbed a palm across his face. God, he didn't know what he wanted anymore. He blinked rapidly, then stared out over the land. It was stark land, not very forgiving. It asked a lot of a man.

But it gave something back, too. It gave a man courage. It gave him self-respect. It gave him the guts to carry on year after year.

Or it crushed him.

The land hadn't crushed Tanner.

His promise to Abby might. Did he dare risk it? Could he manage his feelings long enough to show that same kind of courage where his promise to Abby was concerned?

He stared at Ab's headstone. It was granite. Gray and enduring. He knew it would outlast him, that it would reproach him every day of this life and the next if he didn't at least try.

* * *

The best thing about spring roundup, and something Tanner had never really appreciated until this year, was that when you were thinking about rounding up several hundred head of cattle, you didn't have time to think about anything else.

He didn't have time to brush his teeth or change his socks, much less moon about Maggie MacLeod.

He blessed Abby, considering the rigorous schedule divine intervention of a sort.

Instead of lying awake at night thinking about how Maggie looked in jeans or what it would be like to take her to bed, he worried about which cowboys would be available, which horses they would bring, how he ought to pair them up and send them out, and what sort of devilment the cattle would get into this time.

The advantage to this being his fourth roundup on the Three Bar C was that he was beginning to get a pretty good idea of just what sort of problems he could expect.

For the most part Abigail's herd was an easygoing lot. They didn't take one look at you and head off eighty miles an hour in the other direction. Most of the year, at least. Spring fever, though, seemed to take its toll on them as well.

As docile as they might be when there was just one or two cowboys lurking about, it was as if they had a sixth sense when it came to roundup. They seemed to know just when they were expected to cooperate—and then they did the opposite.

It was Tanner's job to outthink, outsmart and outmaneuver them.

He did this by lying awake at night plotting his strategy, figuring the number of cattle, the number of men, the savvy of their horses, the lay of the land. He threw in variables like temperature, wind, weather and who might not be able to make it at the last minute and whose horse might pull up lame.

And then he tried to think of alternative plans.

He knew as well as the next guy that there was just so far he could get with all the plans and alternatives in the world. But they were consuming, they were necessary and they did keep him from thinking about Maggie MacLeod.

Most of the time.

There was the odd moment, however, that fleeting instant when the sight or sound of her would catch him unawares. It was like being blindsided, knocked flat. One minute he'd be clearheaded and coherent, and the next he'd be fumbling for what he was supposed to be doing or saying or thinking.

"Reckon you might need training wheels for that horse?" Ev asked him finally, the night before the roundup. In the middle of explaining who was coming in the morning, Tanner had caught a glimpse of Maggie in the doorway and had turned so far that he almost fell off when Gambler stepped sideways.

He could feel the hot blood course into his face. "Just, uh, thought I saw something."

"You did," Ev agreed solemnly. Then he grinned and gave Tanner a knowing wink.

Tanner scowled, tugged his hat down, then looked away. He'd been keeping out of Maggie's way ever since he'd made up his mind to stay. It hadn't been too hard, given the amount of work he had to do. But still there were times he couldn't help but run into her. And at those times he did his best to appear as disinterested as possible.

If Maggie thought it was amusing, she didn't let on. Ev did, because Ev saw more than any old man had a right to. But Ev, after Tanner had chewed him out about telling

Maggie about the sheep, was a bit more circumspect. Still, it didn't stop him smirking.

The morning of the roundup dawned clear and cool. Tanner was up well ahead of it. It was still dark when he went to the house to eat. The lights were on and he expected to find Ev already cooking breakfast for the hands as they showed up. He found Maggie.

"Where's Ev?"

"He's got the flu." She filled a plate, and when she turned to hand it to him, he saw dark smudges under her eyes, as if she hadn't slept.

He wanted to ask if she was up to all this, Ev's work as well as her own, but he didn't want to sound concerned. Not about her, anyway. She'd take it wrong.

He took the plate she handed him and set it on the table, then turned and climbed the stairs to the bedrooms. It was the first time he'd been up here since he'd moved out. He walked quietly along the hallway and tapped on the door to Ev's room, then opened it a crack.

Ev was lying huddled in his bed. He moaned, then opened one eye. "Checkin' to make sure I ain't faking it?"

"Of course not," Tanner said, ignoring a twinge of guilt at the accuracy of the remark.

"Hell of a thing to happen," Ev grumbled. "Poor Maggie." He fixed Tanner with a hard look. "I was gonna do most of the cookin' and she was gonna help outside. Reckon we'll be one person short now."

"Somebody'll show up."

"Well, if they don't, don't you go gripin' at her."

"Me?"

Ev snorted. "Don't go soundin' so blessed innocent. You ain't. You ain't hardly had a cheerful word to say to her in weeks."

"I haven't hardly talked to her in weeks!"

"That's exactly what I mean. Well, you talk to her now. You tell her everything's gonna be fine."

Tanner pressed his lips into a thin line.

"Tell her," Ev insisted. He moaned again, grimacing and holding his stomach.

Tanner sighed, tugged on his hat brim and backed out the door.

There were four cowboys packing away breakfast by the time he came back down. He sat at the table and began eating, too. When he'd finished, he took the coffee mug Maggie handed him and met her gaze.

"Thanks for the breakfast. It was good." His eyes flickered to the dishes filled with ham and bacon, eggs and sausage, pancakes and potatoes. "You're doin' fine," he told her, the way Ev had instructed him to.

He wasn't prepared for the smile that lit her face. It was like being socked in the gut. "Thank you," she said. She touched his hand.

For an instant his fingers closed over hers. Then he pulled his hand away, nodded his head, then raised his voice. "I'll be waitin' outside so we can get started."

The day was a blur of activity. By sunup eight crews were fanning out in various directions to round up and bring in the cattle. Only one bunch ran in the wrong direction and had to be regathered. Tanner, watching, felt lucky that that was all they'd screwed up. But he couldn't breathe a sigh of relief. With more than a hundred bawling babies being separated from their mothers, and more than a hundred mooing mother cows looking desperately for their mislaid children, there was plenty of work to be done.

The Three Bar C had always branded in what some people now thought of as "the old-fashioned way," using a regular iron, not a calf table and electric brands as some did now. The calves were all branded, their ears notched, their horns removed with hot lye paste. The bull calves were castrated. All the calves received a seven-way vaccine. It was hot, sweaty, dirty work.

And Maggie was right in the middle of it whenever Tanner looked around.

He'd expected that she'd be in the house fixing the huge meal that would follow the branding. And from what he heard, she'd done her fair share of that. But she was in the thick of things outside, too. Once when he looked over she was sitting on a calf, holding it down for Bates who was using the dehorning paste. Another time when he glanced around she was injecting vaccine into a calf. Still another time he saw her taking a turn with the branding iron.

That was when she looked up and their gazes met. Her auburn hair was coming loose from the band she'd pulled it back in. Tendrils of it stuck to her cheek. She had a dirt smudge on her forehead and nameless muck on the front of her shirt. She looked about as far from a prim schoolteacher as he could imagine. She grinned at him.

In spite of himself, Tanner grinned back. Then, abruptly, he remembered how dangerous his feelings about Maggie were, how easy it would be to pursue her, to want her. He turned back to the corral and yelled at Andy to start bringing in another bunch of calves.

It wasn't until they were almost finished that Tanner noticed John Merritt was there as well. He was on horseback moving the mother cows and their calves back up toward the foothill pastureland.

Tanner stopped next to Andy as he let the last calves run back to their mothers. "What's he doing here?"

"Helping out."

"All the way from Laramie?" Tanner said sarcastically.

Andy glanced at him, surprised. "Maggie called him when Ev got sick in the middle of the night. Wanted to know if he knew anyone else who could help. He said he'd come."

"She didn't ask me. There are plenty of people hereabouts."

"Well—" Andy shifted uncomfortably "—I think maybe Maggie needs to, um, not be turning to you for every little thing."

"I'm the foreman, damn it!"

Andy gave an awkward shrug. "I guess it's just that... she's the boss."

Tanner's teeth came together hard. "Fine," he muttered. "She can get whoever she wants." He gave Gambler a nudge with his heels and set off toward the south pasture, as far away from Merritt as he could manage.

The barbecue was in full swing by the time the cattle were settled to Tanner's satisfaction. The hands and the neighbors and their families were all sitting at tables and on rugs under the cottonwoods, eating, talking and laughing. Even Ev was among them.

"Quick recovery," Tanner said as he came up beside him.

Ev looked faintly sheepish. "Reckon it was somethin' I ate."

"Probably," Tanner said dryly. "Looks like Maggie found you a replacement."

"Sure was nice of him to come all the way up to help out. That's a long drive."

Which was something of an understatement, Tanner thought. His gaze scanned the tables and rugs until he found Merritt. He was, naturally, sitting with Maggie and Andy on a rug near the old shed. They were laughing. Maggie had her head tipped back and Tanner's eyes lingered on the graceful line of her throat. He felt the awareness beginning to pool within him. He shut his eyes, turning away, then grabbed a plate and began to load it with chicken and ribs.

In the old days someone would have had a fiddle and someone else would have brought a guitar, and after the food had been eaten and the talking had slowed, someone would have begun to play, to tempt tired, wornout cowboys to look again at the women in their lives, to tease them into maybe just one dance.

Tonight someone brought out a boom box, someone else turned up the volume and another generation of cowboys started looking around. Some were eager, some were shy. But before long, four couples were dancing in the dirt clearing between the house and the barn. Tanner leaned back against a cottonwood and watched.

One of them was Bates, his head bent close to Amy Lesser's, his arms holding her tight against his angular body. Amy didn't seem to mind. Tanner watched as Andy sidled up to Mary Jean, Bates's sister. She was no proof against Andy's eager grin.

Tanner's gaze slipped toward Maggie. She and Merritt were sitting close together on the blanket, but whether they were actually touching or not, Tanner couldn't tell. His gaze met Maggie's for an instant. Then he looked away.

A moment later a shadow fell across him and he looked up to see her standing there. "We did it," she said. She was smiling.

He knew what she meant. They'd completed the roundup; things had gone well. They should be pleased. He nodded. "Yep."

"Come celebrate with me."

He looked up at her.

She was holding out her hand. "Dance with me."

He swallowed, let his gaze drop slowly, considered the invitation, the desperation with which he wanted to accept it, the probable outcome if he did. He raised his eyes again and met hers and shook his head slowly. "I don't think that would be a good idea."

Maggie's smile faded. Her hand fell. "Whatever you say, Robert," she said after a moment, her voice absolutely toneless. She turned on her heel and walked away.

Tanner looked down at the ground where he sat, plucked at a weed, yanked it out by the roots. "Damn," he muttered under his breath. "Damn it to hell."

Six

He had to drive more than an hour, clear to Casper, before he found what he was looking for.

When he'd left the barbecue, fuming, he hadn't even known what he wanted except to leave, to put as much space as possible between himself and Maggie MacLeod.

Maggie had made the mistake of asking where he was going.

"Leaving," he'd growled as he'd stalked past her. "Or don't you think I've worked hard enough today?"

"Of course you have," she said a little uncertainly, her hand still resting on John Merritt's shoulder.

"Then I'm taking a little well-deserved time off. And that's all you need to know." He didn't care that Maggie, John, Andy, Ev and half of the inhabitants east of the Big Horns stared after him in astonishment.

He took off in a spray of gravel, driving fast and furious, not realizing until he hit the outskirts of Casper exactly what it was he was looking for: an escape—a little nightlife, a little joy, a big opportunity to meet a willing member of the fairer sex.

Another night Tanner might have had enough maturity to walk away from a wet-T-shirt contest.

Tonight it seemed like a good place to start.

The Wildcatter was, as its name indicated, as often frequented by oil-company men as by homegrown Wyoming cowboys. The music was loud, the enthusiasm louder and it was late enough that the highlight of the evening, the wet-T-shirt contest, had begun by the time Tanner got there.

The first contestant was already up on the makeshift platform at the end of the room when the bartender shoved a beer in Tanner's direction. He took a long swallow, then leaned back against the bar to watch.

There were half a dozen contestants. All of them better endowed than Maggie MacLeod. He studied them closely—the two blondes, the redhead, the three brunettes—and wondered what it would be like to dance with them, kiss them, run his hands over them.

The frustration that had been growing for weeks—no, months—rampaged in him. He watched as the women came forward in response to the whistles and hand claps. He studied their assets as the official "wetter" used a spray bottle to reveal them. He tried to imagine taking any one of them to a motel and doing what Maggie and John Merritt were probably doing at this very moment.

His jaw clamped shut.

Suddenly his line of vision was obscured. A leggy blonde brushed up against his arm. "Hi, honey." She smiled at him, her voice sultry, attractive and definitely inviting.

"Evenin'." He glanced at her. She didn't have the obvious attributes of the contestants on the platform at the end of the room, but even she probably had more to show off than Maggie had.

"Buy me a beer, cowboy?" she suggested.

He signaled to the bartender. The blonde edged closer to him. "I'm Carrie. Who're you?"

"Tanner." He finished his beer. The bartender poured him another. Carrie rubbed her cheek against the denim of his jacket. He remembered how he flinched away from the desire that shot through him every time Maggie touched him. He tried to find that desire here. He tried to imagine taking Carrie to a motel, easing off her skintight pink shirt and the rest of her clothes, laying her down and making love to her.

He'd never had any trouble imagining doing that to Maggie—even when he didn't want to.

He felt more than disinterest now. He gulped his beer and looked desperately back at the girls on the platform, trying to muster up interest in one of them. From the stamping and shouting and whistling going on around him, it was pretty clear that the other men weren't having any trouble relating to their considerable charms.

Carrie pouted. "They may have more than me," she said when she noticed where his gaze had focused, "but boobs aren't everything, are they, sugar?" She gave Tanner a coy smile and brushed against him again.

He cleared his throat and shifted his weight. "Er, no. I . . . reckon not."

She reached for his hand, toying with his fingers. "Why don't you let me show you what else I've got."

He couldn't.

God help him, even faced with an outright invitation, he couldn't say yes.

Damned if he knew why.

His hormones thought he'd lost his senses. His body clamored at his betrayal. The frustrating pressure in his loins told him he'd lost his mind. But for all that certain parts of him frantically craved the release he was sure this woman could provide, he couldn't take her arm and walk out with her. He couldn't contemplate going to a motel room with her. He couldn't think about having sex with her.

Because he couldn't stop thinking about Maggie.

He tipped his head back and drained his glass, then looked at Carrie and shook his head. "Can't," he said. "Thanks, but no."

Carrie looked at him, taken aback. "No?"

Tanner gave a rueful shrug. "Not tonight," he said. "I...gotta get going." Shoving some bills toward the bartender, he gave Carrie a quick nod and strode out of the bar without looking back.

The spring night had cooled considerably and served as a temporary balm to his overheated body, but it did nothing for the frustration that had been tormenting him for weeks.

There was only one thing that would really ease it.

One woman.

And he hadn't a snowball's chance in hell of making love with Maggie MacLeod and walking away. It was more than his life was worth to even think about it.

He flung himself into the truck, flicked on the engine and jammed it into gear. In his mind's eye he could see Carrie's smiling come-on, could feel the pressing need even now against the fabric of his jeans. He remembered the sight of Maggie as she laughed at Merritt's words, her hand on Merritt's arm as they danced, the possessive curve of Merritt's arm around her.

If Maggie felt any frustrations tonight, Tanner was sure John Merritt was solving them for her.

He headed up the highway, furious.

It was past two by the time he turned onto the gravel road that led into the Three Bar C. His fury hadn't abated, nor had his frustration. But he slowed down anyway because he didn't want to announce his return with any more noise than he had to. He even turned off his headlights as he came into the ranch yard. He looked for Merritt's car.

He didn't see it, but that didn't mean he wasn't still here. Maggie might have had him pull it into the shed. Or—and this thought made his stomach hurt even worse—she might have even left with him.

There was still a light on in the kitchen and another on the back porch—as if she'd left it on to light up her return.

He got out of the truck and started toward the bunkhouse. Habit alone made him stop at the barn. In his hurry to be gone this evening, he hadn't taken the time to check the two cows that still hadn't calved. He wanted at least to look in on the horses.

He did it quickly and casually, until he came to the last stall.

Sunny wasn't there.

Tanner stared at the empty stall, then shook his head, trying to clear it of the two beers he'd had in Casper, trying to figure out where he'd gone. Sunny's saddle and bridle were gone, too.

No one rode Sunny. Except Maggie.

She couldn't have. Wouldn't have, he assured himself. She had no reason.

He rejected the notion even as his mind was beginning to grapple with the unpleasant truth: she very well might have. Especially if she knew he hadn't checked the cattle.

Maybe the cattle had nothing to do with it. Maybe she'd gone off for a moonlight ride with Merritt.

He sure as hell didn't want to go looking for her if that was what she was doing.

But what if she hadn't?

It was the middle of the night. She ought to have returned by now. Unless . . .

Quick as he could, Tanner saddled Gambler and led him out.

He headed toward the pasture just east of the ridge, the one where he'd put the two remaining pregnant heifers. He had no way of knowing if that was where she'd headed. He had no way of knowing if she was with Merritt. He'd feel like a complete fool if she was.

He couldn't stop himself.

There was precious little moonlight to see by. He opened the gate and pulled out his flashlight and scanned the countryside, searching for any sign of Maggie or the horse.

Nothing.

Nowhere.

Not until he came over a rise and played the light along the edge of a stand of trees. For an instant its arc caught Sunny in its beam.

Before he could call out, he heard a voice. "Robert! Over here." She sounded frantic.

Tanner gritted his teeth. He played the flashlight over the area, looking for her. At least there was only one horse. But what if she was hurt? He spurred Gambler across the field toward the sound of her voice.

"What in the hell are you doing?" he began, swinging out of the saddle.

"Help me."

There was a thread of panic in her voice that squelched his anger. With the help of the flashlight he found her crouched on the ground, her arm in the business end of a laboring heifer.

"Thank God you're here! She's having a lot of trouble with this calf. It's coming out all wrong. Or rather, it isn't coming out at all." Her voice quavered slightly. She sounded exhausted, but determined.

Tanner crouched beside her. "Let me see." He cursed himself for his selfish desertion of duty. He was the one who should have been out here tonight, not Maggie.

She shifted aside to make room for him, moving to soothe the cow as she had done the last time. "Shh now, sweetie," she crooned. "Everything will be fine. Robert's here."

As if he was going to make things all right. Tanner's jaw clenched. He checked the position of the heifer.

"Don't get your hopes up," he muttered, tossing off his jacket. He hadn't brought his rope, so he pulled his belt out of the loops, then braced himself.

He supposed he was lucky. This calf was smaller than the last one he'd had trouble with, and the cow hadn't been in labor as long. But it took some work to get its head forward and in position and the belt around its feet. Then he settled his own feet against the heifer and pulled on the belt while the cow strained to deliver her burden.

"Here she comes!" Maggie cried.

And the next moment he had a messy, bloody, squirming calf in his lap.

"Oh, Robert! Oh, heavens!" Maggie exclaimed. She was laughing, exulting as the calf wriggled in his arms and he lifted it to place it in front of the mother.

"Thank God," he muttered.

"Thank *you*. I knew you could do it," Maggie said, her voice warm and approving. "It's fantastic."

Tanner grunted. "It was luck." By rights he should've lost the calf and the heifer. He sure as hell didn't deserve any praise.

"I'm so relieved you came when you did," Maggie said now, crouching next to him, watching as the cow licked her calf.

"I should never have left," Tanner muttered. He finished with the afterbirth and hauled himself to his feet. "I should've been here when she started."

"It was your time off."

"I shouldn't have taken it."

"You deserved some time off. I agreed to it," she reminded him.

"It was my job," Tanner said doggedly. He shook his head. "I'm sorry. You better get yourself a new foreman."

Maggie looked up at him, shocked. She scrambled to her feet. "Don't be ridiculous. What sort of nonsense is that?"

"It's not nonsense. It's called fulfilling your responsibilities. I didn't fulfill mine. I'd fire anyone who let me down like this." He met her gaze, grateful the darkness covered at least some of the shame he felt.

It was the same guilt all over again, the same guilt that had assailed him when Clare had lost their child and he'd been nowhere around. The calf hadn't been quite so unlucky—no thanks to him.

"Well, it's a good thing you're not me, then," Maggie said at last. "Isn't it?"

He didn't answer.

"Robert, really. It's okay. You were here." She laid a hand on his arm. He tried not to flinch away. Her touch could undo him and he knew it. He wasn't up to fighting her right now.

"I might not have been. I showed lousy judgment and you know it."

Maggie just looked at him. "This isn't just about the calf, is it?"

"Leave it, Maggie."

She sighed. "If you say so. But I say you're allowed a lapse."

"I don't—"

"I don't care what you say," Maggie went on firmly. "You came when it mattered."

"But—"

"That's enough, Robert. Come on. You're a mess. You need to get cleaned up."

"Not now." He couldn't ride back with her now. "I'll be along."

"I'll wait for you."

He shook his head. "No. You've done your share. And mine," he added heavily.

"I don't mind wait—"

"No." His voice was flat, brooking no argument, and Maggie must have realized he wasn't going to be talked around.

"You're an ornery, stubborn, pigheaded cowboy," she told him.

He nodded. "Thank you, ma'am."

She dimpled and gave the brim of his hat a tug. "Hurry home," she said softly, then mounted her horse and started toward the road that led to the house.

Tanner watched her go. She was perhaps thirty yards from him when he called after her, "How come Merritt didn't come with you?"

He could have kicked himself the moment the words were out of his mouth even though he knew he couldn't have stopped them. Nor could he help the surge of elation he felt when Maggie turned in the saddle and called back to him, "He left before midnight."

It was a cool night for skinny-dipping. The water running down from the mountains was almost pure melted snow. The shower back in the bunkhouse sounded a lot more tempting. But the drumming of the water in the shower stall would wake Andy, asleep on the other side of the thin-walled partition.

Anyway, Tanner thought as he tied Gambler to a cottonwood and headed toward the creek, a little cold creek water might just possibly shock some sense into him. God knew he needed some.

The swiftly moving creek was almost twenty feet wide and perhaps three feet deep. There was a swimming hole farther south, but he didn't have time to ride there.

Besides, he wasn't here for swimming. He was here to wash off the remains of the calf's birth and to dampen, literally, his sexual frustration.

Tanner tugged off his boots and socks, his jacket and shirt and jeans. If Maggie had stayed he'd have kept his shorts on.

If Maggie had stayed...! There was a laugh.

He wouldn't be anywhere near this creek in his underwear if Maggie had stayed with him. That would have been asking for trouble.

He stripped off his shorts and T-shirt and dropped them by his jacket. Then he picked up the clothes the calf had mucked up and carried them to the creek.

The cool night breeze made him shiver. The icy water shocked him. He bent, scrubbing his clothes against the rocks, swishing them in the water, scrubbing them some more and finally rinsing them. Wringing them in his hands, he carried them back to the bank and spread them on the grass. If there was any desire left in him after he plunged back in the icy creek, those clothes would take care of it on the way home.

He turned and headed back into the creek, ducking under, shuddering as the frigid water enveloped him, yet grateful for the ache it shot through him. It was an ache that would blot out his desire for Maggie MacLeod. His body might not enjoy it as much as it would have enjoyed a tumble in the sheets with the girl from the bar, but his mind and his emotions would be happier.

He didn't know how long he stayed in the creek. Long enough so that all those surging feelings of desire were well and truly cooled, long enough so that his skin felt numb and his fingers shriveled.

He wasn't cold now so much as anesthetized. But when at last he stood and made his way carefully across the slick rocks to the bank, the cold breeze smote him.

He grabbed his jacket and blotted himself dry. Then he picked up his T-shirt and pulled it over his head and stepped into his shorts. Then he reached for his soggy jeans.

"I've brought you some dry ones."

He jumped a foot, two feet—damn, he didn't know how high.

"M-Maggie?" he croaked, glancing around wildly.

There was a rustling from a thicket and Maggie stepped into the moonlight, holding out a pair of jeans.

"I saw you head for the creek. I thought you might be going to wash off. So when I got back to the house I went down to the bunkhouse and got you some dry things." She stopped, still holding the jeans, standing perhaps five feet from him.

The cold water had done no good at all.

One word in Maggie's soft tones, one look from Maggie's green eyes, and all Tanner's hormones were standing at attention again. Literally.

He muttered something desperate under his breath.

"What?" Maggie's own voice had a faint, breathless quality. She stepped closer. Her hand, still holding the jeans, dropped to her side. She ran her tongue lightly over her lips. Her wide eyes caught him as surely as he'd ever caught a deer in the sight of his gun.

Tanner's breath lodged in his throat.

She took another step. And another.

And then, when she stopped so close that their breath mingled and her breasts and his chest nearly touched, he couldn't help himself.

He bent his head and, trembling, touched his lips to hers. He drank of her sweetness, tasted her, urged her mouth to open for him, to let him in. He didn't stop to think. God knew he'd been thinking far too much. For weeks all he'd been able to do was think. And it hadn't done him one bit of good. He'd certainly never been able to forget.

From the moment he'd lain in the corral dirt and opened his eyes to see her standing over him, he'd wanted her.

He wanted her still.

And though he knew with just that one tiny shred of rational common sense that was left to him that what he wanted was wrong for both of them, right this instant he couldn't help himself.

He needed to hold her, to touch her, to taste her. He needed it with every fiber of his being, with every singing nerve, and every clamoring cell.

And Maggie didn't resist. On the contrary, she dropped the jeans and wrapped her arms around him, ran her hands up under the damp T-shirt against his back, stroking his shivering, burning flesh, making him shudder, making him need. He thrust himself against her, knowing it was all too obvious how much he desired her. There was no hope of denying it now.

Her fingers threaded through his hair, her lips melded with his. Her tongue slipped inside his mouth and sent him soaring with desire. He held her to him in the cradle of his thighs, reveled in the brush of her worn denim jeans against his bare legs. Her hands skimmed down his back again, toyed with the waistband of his shorts. He arched forward, pressing his arousal against her, moving, throbbing, needing.

"Yes," Maggie whispered. "Oh, yes." She feathered little kisses all over his face while he did the same to her, then their mouths met again with hungry desperation. "I love you, Robert. I love you."

The words cracked like a bullwhip against his conscience, jerking him back to reality, to a time larger than now, to a world that would go on after his hunger had been sated.

With every bit of resolve that he could muster, Tanner wrenched himself back, snatched his mouth from hers, held her body away from his. He gulped in great lungfuls of air, tried to calm the stampede of his heart, the thrum of the blood in his veins.

"Stop," he said hoarsely. "Got to stop."

Maggie stared back at him, dazed, as hungry as he, hurt etching her face, confusion filling her eyes. Her lips were parted in a tiny O so tempting that he wanted to kiss her again—and again—and never let her go.

But it couldn't happen. He couldn't *let* it happen.

"It's all right," Maggie assured him.

"It *isn't!*"

"But I do, you know, Robert," she said softly.

He gave his head a little shake, confused. "Do?"

"Love you."

He shook his head fiercely. "No. You don't. You can't! You don't know..." he said, his voice tight with anguish. He turned away from her, snagged the dry jeans off the ground and, stumbling, tugged them on, wincing as he zipped them up.

"You don't know," he repeated.

"So tell me." She looked at him with gentleness, with warmth, with all the care he'd craved for so long.

He shut his eyes, felt the cold air heaving in and out of his lungs, tried to get a grip on himself, didn't have much luck.

So tell me.

It sounded so simple. It was so damn hard.

He pulled on the shirt she'd brought him, too. His fingers fumbled with the buttons, buying himself time. But he knew he owed her some explanation, at least.

"You want a home," he began at last. "You said that from the first." His voice was ragged. He cleared his throat.

"Yes."

"I can't...do that."

"Why not?"

"I don't know!" he said, anguished. "Maybe it's a genetic failing. No, probably not. My old man seemed to have managed. Hell, maybe it's just me!"

"But how do you know you can't?" Maggie persisted.

"Because...because I've tried."

She looked at him, waiting, not speaking.

"I've been married."

There. He'd said it. Told her what he hadn't told anyone since he'd left Colorado. "And you can ask her," he went on bitterly. "She'll tell you I was lousy at it. She'll tell you I was never there when she needed me! Hell—" he took an angry swipe at his eyes "—you think I was negligent with this calf tonight. Clare was pregnant. She was having our baby. And I wasn't even there when she lost him!"

He heard the sharp intake of Maggie's breath, then felt her move close, put her arms around him. He should have shoved her away. God knew he didn't deserve her comfort. But he couldn't do it. He just stood there, trembling, aching, suddenly hurting more now for the loss of his son than he'd hurt fourteen years before.

"Can you tell me?" she asked softly.

And so he told her about coming home that night, about being relieved when Clare wasn't there. He told her everything about that day. It didn't come out at once. It came out in harsh, aching chunks. But he managed it all—until he got to the baby.

"I never—" his voice sounded harsh and strange even to him "—I never even saw him!"

It was the cry he'd never been able to share with Clare. He'd tried to be strong for her, to be tough and silent and forbearing, not saying a word lest she think he blamed her when he'd blamed only himself.

"If only," he'd said to himself a million times as he fixed fences, herded cattle, doctored pink eye, cut hay. *If only.*

But all the if onlys in the world couldn't bring back the son he'd never known, the home he'd hoped to make.

For years he'd pretended it didn't matter. Cowboying was enough. Moving on was fine with him.

Because he'd never given himself another choice. Meeting Maggie had forced him to face what he'd told himself he had no right to, forced him to confront the dreams he'd thought were dead.

He pressed his face against her shoulder, felt a shudder shake him. Her arms tightened around him, held him fast and made him wish—*Oh, God, how they made him wish*—that he could risk a second chance.

Finally he pulled back, scrubbing at the dampness around his eyes with his hand, embarrassed. "Sorry," he muttered. He jammed his fists into the pockets of his jeans, ducked his head. "I shouldn't have done that."

"On the contrary," Maggie said softly, her hand still on his arm, not letting him go. "I think it's high time you did."

Tanner cleared his throat. "Maybe. But it . . . shouldn't have been you."

"No," Maggie said. "It probably should have been . . . your wife. You never told her, did you?"

"I couldn't. We didn't talk. We just . . ." He flushed, remembering what Clare's primary attraction was. "We were kids. Being married at that age, for us at least, was a joke. On us. We didn't know what we were doing. I had great hopes." He gave an ironic laugh at the young naive fool he had been. "But when—" his voice caught in his throat "—when the baby was born early, when he died . . . everything just . . . fell apart. I couldn't stop it."

"I know you, Robert. I'm sure you tried."

"Did I?" How many years had he wondered about that? He gave a harsh half sob, half laugh. "Sometimes I think I was just glad to get out, glad that he died!" He looked at her, expecting to see mirrored in her face all the self-loathing he'd lived with for so many years. His own anguish was unbearable. "Do you have any idea what it's like, thinking you're the kind of person who's glad his own kid died?"

And then she was holding him again and he really was crying this time. There was no way he could hide it or pretend he'd gotten something in his eye or anything else. He felt like the world's biggest jerk, but he couldn't help it.

Maggie didn't try to stop him. She just held him, rubbed her hands over his back, kissed his cheek, his ear, his hair. Then she fished in her pocket and handed him a handkerchief, as if it was a perfectly normal thing that he'd just done.

"Lots of guys break down and bawl in your arms?" Tanner said after he'd cleared his throat and could talk again. She might not be embarrassed for him, but he was embarrassed as hell.

"John did."

Tanner stiffened at her mention of Merritt. "When his marriage fell apart?" he asked gruffly.

"No. When we were in college his mother died."

"Oh." He felt like an even bigger fool. "I'm sorry. I didn't mean—"

Maggie laid a hand on his arm. "John and I are friends, Robert. We have been for a long time."

"You don't have to explain. It's none of my business."

"Yes, it is," Maggie told him, "because I love you."

"Don't say things like that." He turned away and, grabbing his wet clothes and pulling on his jacket, headed for his horse. Doggedly, Maggie followed him. "It's true. I think I fell in love with you the day I came. I watched you ride that black mare, watched her buck you off over and over—"

"Swell," Tanner muttered.

"—And I watched you get right back on. I admired you tremendously. You had guts, stamina, commitment."

He swung into the saddle. "Yeah, where horses are concerned, I'm a regular marvel."

"You sell yourself short."

His teeth clenched. "I see myself realistically. Horses are one thing, love is something else. I tried. It doesn't work. *I* don't work."

"You were scarcely more than a child!"

"Just the same," he insisted stubbornly, "I failed."

"And you won't try again?" She stood there looking up at him, offering him her heart. He could hear it in her voice, see it in her eyes. She offered him dreams and hopes, the promise of a future that he didn't dare contemplate no matter how much he wanted to.

He shook his head. "I . . . can't," he whispered.

Her chin jutted. "Can't? Or won't? Don't you want to, Robert? Or are you afraid?"

He met her gaze defiantly. Then, seeing the love in hers, he looked away.

"Don't push me, Maggie," he said, then touched his heels to the horse and rode off.

Seven

So now she knew.

It wasn't something he'd ever wanted to talk about. Certainly not to Maggie. But maybe it was just as well.

Now she wouldn't be thinking she loved him. Maggie MacLeod was no fool. It wouldn't take her long to realize she'd had a close call, that a relationship with a man like him would be the biggest mistake she could ever make.

Tanner knew he ought to be glad it had happened. But sometimes—just sometimes—when he saw her watching him from a distance, looking at him sadly, it hurt. He tried not to think about it. He tried to do his job, to teach Andy, to stay out of Maggie's way.

Why not? They had nothing to talk about except the ranch, and if he managed things right, he didn't have to say much to her about that. If she thought he was avoiding her, well, he was.

And now she ought to understand why.

But she looked at him so unhappily. Damn, did she think he wanted to be this sort of man?

He was grateful when the time came for him and Andy to take the cattle up to the summer pasture. It would require several days, days when he wouldn't have to see her watching him from a distance, days that his gut wouldn't clench at the sight of her, and his heart wouldn't ache because now she knew the worst.

Ordinarily this trip was made during one of Tanner's favorite times of the year. He looked forward to being out on the range, to the wilderness, to the solitude, to the genial companionship of the one or two men who came with him.

But going with Andy made it hard. The boy had learned a lot. He was quick and eager and determined, always asking questions, always trying to help.

Like his sister. Too damned much like his sister. It was bad enough having Maggie constantly in the back of his mind. It was worse having Andy along to remind him even more of her.

Tanner knew he was being curt with him, that Andy didn't know why, that he thought it was something he'd done that was making Tanner stay away from him as much as he could.

Tanner couldn't help it. He excused it by telling himself it was better for the kid to learn how to handle things on his own.

"Remember," he said, sending Andy in the other direction. "You learn by doing. I can't do it for you."

And if Andy sometimes looked at him a little warily and a little sadly, too, well, that was just too bad.

The kid was learning. He was like his sister that way, too. Tanner knew that Maggie would have made Abby proud of her. She'd be proud of Andy, too. He didn't stop to consider what she'd think of him.

Watching the kid now, as they herded the last cow across the track and up through the forest into the high, verdant meadow, Tanner thought he'd done all right.

Andy shut the last gate, then leaned back in the saddle and took off his hat, surveying with proprietary pride the settling herd. He rubbed the sweat from his forehead with one grimy hand and grinned, then glanced over at Tanner. His gaze was still a little wary, as if he was unsure of Tanner's approval.

"That's it?" he asked.

"That's it."

"So we did it?"

"We did it." Tanner rode over to the creek and slipped out of the saddle to dip his neck scarf in the water and wipe his face. The icy water trickled down his neck.

Andy joined him and did the same, then he clapped his hat back on his head and whooped loud and long.

"What was that for?"

"'Cause I'm finally a cowboy." Andy grinned, tasting the word, savoring it on his tongue. Then he stopped and glanced hesitantly at Tanner. "Aren't I?"

Tanner nodded. "You could say that."

"Would you say it?"

Tanner looked at the young, freckled face, at the green eyes so like Maggie's. In them he saw hope and faith in the future, purity, innocence and self-esteem. All the things he'd once had. He hoped to hell Andy got to keep them. "Yeah, Andy, I would."

"It's 'cause of you, Tanner. Learn by doing. I do everything you do."

"Don't, for God's sake, do everything I do," Tanner said gruffly, swinging back into the saddle.

Which was good advice, because moments later, he fell off his horse.

"Tanner what?" Ev's eyes bugged. He stared, stupefied, first at Andy, then at Tanner riding into the yard slowly, his face white and pained, his left arm wrapped tightly against his chest and held in place with Andy's shirt.

"The cinch broke," Tanner muttered, embarrassed beyond belief.

He saw Maggie come out on the porch, take one look at him and start running. He cursed under his breath.

"Hold his horse," she instructed Billy, then she looked at Tanner. "I'll help you down,"

"I don't need help." He clenched his teeth, clutched the saddle horn for balance and swung down. White-hot pain shot through his arm and shoulder as his foot hit the ground. He couldn't stop the expletive that passed his lips as Maggie's arm slipped around him.

"Easy," she soothed. "Give me a hand, Ev. We'll get him to the truck."

Tanner made a feeble effort to shake them both off. But he was light-headed, almost groggy with pain. He winced as Ev helped him into the pickup.

"Where to?" Maggie asked Ev.

"Casper. He's prob'ly broke something."

"I dislocated my shoulder."

"Again?" Ev grumbled.

"Does he do it often?" Maggie asked.

"Usually I can pop it back in. This time I... couldn't."

Maggie turned to Ev. "Call ahead and tell them we're coming."

"Ev can—" Tanner began.

But Maggie just slid behind the wheel. "Let's go."

In terms of sheer pain, the trip to Casper was less awful than riding down the mountain. But sitting next to Maggie for an hour, trying desperately not to disgrace himself by puking or fainting, was sheer hell.

He was just congratulating himself on having made it when Maggie opened the door of the truck in front of the emergency entrance and he put his feet on the ground. The world begin to shift. From a long way off he saw Maggie move toward him and heard her say, "Wait a sec—"

The world didn't wait. It came up to meet his face.

There was apparently no end to the ways he could make an ass of himself in front of Maggie. But why, he wondered, if he was going to faint, didn't he have the good sense to stay out for the duration?

Why did he have to come around as nurses and orderlies were picking him up, as Maggie was saying, "Mind his shoulder," as some helpful busybody was unbuttoning his shirt and undoing the snap of his jeans to help him breathe?

He struggled against them, but the pain stopped him dead. He sagged and shut his eyes as they lay him on the cart.

"Has he fainted again?" Maggie asked.

He wished to God he had.

"Take him into the examining room," he heard one of the nurses command. "And if you'll just come with me, I need some information...."

And that, Tanner thought, got rid of Maggie. He breathed easier for the first time since she'd come out of the house.

He felt himself being rolled into one of the examining rooms. The door shut. Through his closed lids he could sense the glare of the overhead lights.

Nurses bustled, muttered and clanked things. Drawers opened and shut. Then the door creaked again. Heavy footsteps approached.

"Well, hell, Tanner," said a jovial masculine voice. "You again. Thought I told you I'd seen enough of you this year."

"Hullo, Brent." He didn't bother to open his eyes. "I tried to put it back myself."

Brent Walker had done his share of stitching and patching Tanner during the past three years. He'd put the shoulder back before, too.

"Roll this way." Brent patted the side away from Tanner's damaged shoulder, and carefully Tanner did as he was told, until he was lying on his face. He still hadn't opened his eyes. He didn't need to. He knew what was going to happen.

Brent took hold of his arm. "Just a little shot to make it hurt less. Marybeth?" More footsteps; a stool moved. Then the cool swab touched his back. A needle pricked and stung.

After a few moments Brent said, "Okay, Tanner. Ready? Hang loose now."

Two pairs of hands held him steady. He knew exactly what would happen next and braced himself. He dug his face into the starched pillowcase and wished for purchase for the toes of his boots. Cool fingers touched his right hand. He gripped them fiercely, felt Brent move his arm, pull and—

"Hell!"

Involuntary tears sprang to his eyes. He crushed the hand he held in his.

"All done," Brent said cheerfully. "You can open your eyes now."

Tanner did.

Maggie was sitting on a stool just inches from him, her fingers locked tight in the grip of his hand.

He muttered an oath under his breath. "S-sorry." He tried to loosen his fingers. They barely worked.

She chafed them lightly with hers. "It's all right. Are you okay now?"

"I'm fine." He shifted around and started to sit up. The world was still unsteady.

"Take it easy," Brent said, catching him by his good arm. "You don't want to go fainting again."

"I'm not going to faint," Tanner said irritably. "I was just a little light-headed earlier. It'd been awhile since I ate."

"Right." Brent handed him a sling. "Wear it for a week. And sit still. You're not finished yet. While we've got you here, we might as well let these lovely ladies clean you up."

Tanner didn't know what he meant until one of the nurses eased his shirt clear off and two others started dabbing at his face and his neck and a spot on his head. Then he realized that when the cinch gave he'd suffered a bit more damage than just his shoulder. He was scraped from his neck to his ribs. He tried to sit stoically under their ministrations. Maggie watched avidly.

"You don't have to stay," he said.

"I don't mind."

"I thought you were filling out forms."

"I don't know much of your personal history."

She knew more than anyone else, Tanner thought.

"Anyway, they said you could do it after." She didn't move an inch. She waited until they were finished cleaning him up, until they had rebuttoned his shirt, trussed him up in the sling and, to his chagrin, had even refastened his jeans for him. Then, after he'd filled out the forms and swallowed two of the pain pills Brent gave him, she pocketed the rest and followed him out, like a herd dog with a balky steer.

"He'll be sore for a few days," Brent told her just as if Tanner were her child. "Looks like he whacked his head, too. Have someone keep an eye on him for the next day or so."

"See I don't fall off my horse again?" Tanner growled.

"You won't be on a horse for a few days," Brent said firmly. He turned back to Maggie. "Make him sleep, but wake him up every few hours. You got to keep an eye on this guy. Last spring it was his knee. This is the third or fourth time with the shoulder. Don't know if he's accident prone or what."

Tanner shot him a dirty look.

"He's a pretty good horseman usually. But, well—" Brent grinned "—I think every now and then he figures he needs a little TLC."

"The hell I do!"

"And with such a pretty new boss—"

"I still got one good arm. I can break your nose for you, Walker!"

"He gets a mite nasty when you call him on it, though," Brent said without missing a beat. "Humor him a bit. He won't malinger long."

"I've never—!"

"Shh, Robert." Maggie took his good arm and drew him along toward the exit. She was smiling at him, amusement lighting her eyes. "He's just teasing."

Tanner didn't think it was funny.

"Robert?" he heard Brent say behind him.

Maggie glance over her shoulder. "That's his name."

Brent cocked his head. "Well, I'll be damned."

* * *

The pain pills made him groggy. He caught his eyes closing and his head slipping sideways half a dozen times at least. He jerked upright again, wincing, damned if he was going to fall asleep and wake up to find his head on Maggie's shoulder. Or worse, and probably more likely, her lap.

"You ought to rest," Maggie said.

"I'll rest when I get back."

"Ev will make up the bed in Abigail's room. It won't take long."

"I'm not sleeping there! I live in the bunkhouse."

"You're supposed to have someone to watch you."

"Andy can watch me. He lives there, too." There was no way he was staying in the house with her. It was bad enough seeing her at a distance.

"Don't be ridiculous."

"I'm staying in the bunkhouse. If you don't like it fire me. If you won't fire me, I'll quit." He glared at her, defying her to argue with him.

For a minute he thought she was going to. But finally she sighed. "Fine. Be muleheaded. Stay in the bunkhouse."

"I will."

"Robert?"

"Uh?"

"Robert?" A hand touched his arm.

"Wha—"

"Robert, can you open your eyes?"

He blinked, dazed, into the darkness. Where the hell was he? "Who?"

"It's me," the voice said. "Maggie."

Maggie? Agitated, he started to sit up, then the soreness stabbed him again and he sagged back against the pillows, blinking up at the woman who bent over him in the darkness. "Wha' the hell are you doing here?"

"Checking on you."

"Andy—"

"Andy has to get up earlier than I do. He's doing your work now, too, remember?"

Tanner scowled. "Thanks for reminding me."

"Sorry. Are you all right? Do you need more pain pills?"

"No." Which was a lie.

"Doesn't it hurt?"

"Like hell."

"Well, then—"

"I don't want 'em. They make me stupid."

"Oh, is that what's causing it?"

He frowned. "I don't like the way they make me feel."

"But can you sleep without them?"

"I could if people didn't keep wakin' me up. Go away."

She didn't say anything, nor did she move. His shoulder was throbbing. His head ached. And he knew damned well she wasn't going to leave without stuffing the pills down his throat.

"Oh, hell. Give 'em to me then."

At least she didn't say "I told you so." She got a glass of water, then held it to his lips while he took the pills.

"If you need anything else, just call."

"I won't bother Andy." He would have rolled over and turned his back on her, but his shoulder hurt too much.

She woke him one more time before sunup. This time he was quicker coming around and he knew right away who it was.

"Damn, you're taking this serious, aren't you?" He glowered at her in the predawn dimness.

"Just checking." She smiled. She looked like an angel again. He shut his eyes.

"Wakin' Andy, too, probably," he muttered.

"Andy's getting plenty of sleep."

"So can you. Leave me alone." This time he did roll over, even though it hurt like hell.

So he was rude. So he shouldn't have been so abrupt with her when she was only trying to help. But damn it, he didn't need her help! He needed her to stay away.

"G'way," he muttered.

"What?"

"Are you still here?"

She leaned over him again. "What's wrong?"

"You, damn it. Hovering. Go away and let me sleep."

She touched his hair lightly. A shiver ran through him. "Go to sleep then, Robert."

"Tanner," he muttered. "Tanner, damm it."

"Whatever you say, darling," Maggie whispered.

Oh God, were those her lips touching his hair?

The sun was up the next time he opened his eyes. This time Maggie didn't wake him. She was asleep herself. In Andy's bed.

Tanner blinked, disbelieving. He shook his head, felt it pound, a result of the fall and the painkillers. But even through the fog that was his brain, the image didn't change.

Maggie was there.

He eased over onto his right side and lay shoved up against the pillows, just looking at her. He knew she shouldn't be here. A part of him was furious that she was. And another part of him, the part that had for so long ached after her, simply wanted to look his fill.

The temptation was too much for him. She lay curled on her side facing him, one hand gripping the blanket, hugging it against her breasts, the other tucked under her cheek. Her gorgeous hair was loose and tousled, dark auburn against the white pillowcase. Her lips were slightly parted, curving in a tiny smile. Tanner's tongue touched his own lips, which felt suddenly dry.

There were dark circles under her eyes, as if she hadn't had enough sleep. No surprise there. She'd been bouncing up like a jackrabbit all night to see if he was all right.

And he hadn't even known she was there.

Ev and Andy had helped him to the bunkhouse. Ev had helped him get undressed. Andy had gone up to get some supper, offering to bring him some. But Tanner had said he just wanted to sleep—and he had, not even remembering when Andy came back.

Obviously, Andy hadn't come back. Maggie had.

And had slept less than three feet away from him all night. Nursemaiding him. And unless he got up and got himself dressed before she awoke, she'd probably insist on dressing him, too.

He eased his aching body around so that he sat on the side of the bed. His head felt as if some blacksmith had set up shop inside and was working three shifts. He would've liked to sit there and get his bearings, but he knew she'd wake up and find him if he did.

He hauled himself to his feet, grimacing when the bedsprings creaked, expecting any moment to see Maggie's wide green eyes flick open. Thank heaven she merely sighed and shifted slightly, then puckered her lips as if she were giving someone a kiss.

Tanner averted his gaze. Then, with his arm against his chest, he walked carefully toward the bathroom.

He would have liked to take a shower, but he was sure the noise of the spraying water against the shower stall would wake Maggie. So he contented himself with brushing his teeth and slopping water on a cloth and scrubbing his face and torso, all the while trying not to do more than he had to with his sore shoulder.

When he'd finally dried off, he crept quietly back into the bunk room and reached for his jeans.

"I hope that doesn't mean you're planning on getting dressed."

He jerked around, swearing from the pain in his shoulder. Maggie was still lying on her side, but those wide green eyes were open now and fastened right on him. He grabbed his jeans from off the chair.

"What the— Of course it does!" He bent over, lifting one foot, trying to stick it into his pant leg, a difficult business since he could hold the jeans with only one hand. He lost his balance.

Maggie leapt out of bed wearing an oversize T-shirt and nothing else. "Sit down!" She grabbed him by his right arm and hauled him down onto the bed next to her, so close their bare thighs touched.

Out of the corner of his eye he could see the rise and fall of her breasts beneath the thin cotton. It wasn't something he should have noticed. Not if he wanted to keep his sanity. Both of them were breathing too damn hard.

"Go back to bed, Robert," she said after a moment. "You need the rest."

"Hell of a lot of rest I'm going to get with you waltzing around the bunkhouse half naked!"

Color flamed in her cheeks. "I was not waltzing! I was trying to take care of you."

"I don't need taking care of."

"Right. You're so tough and so capable and so perfectly fine on your own, aren't you?"

"I try," he grated.

"And you're determined to be that way forever."

"I have to be, and you know it."

"I don't." She touched his knee and his whole body stirred in response.

"Stop it," he said through his teeth.

"I don't want to stop it. I love you."

"What are you trying to do to me?"

"Get inside those walls you've built up around you. Break them down. Set you free." There it was again, her heart right there in her eyes, ripe for the taking.

"Damn it, Maggie!" He raked trembling fingers through his hair. "How the hell long do you think I'm going to be able to go on resisting?"

"I don't know," she said softly. "How long are you?" A faint line of color touched her cheekbones, but she didn't look away. And then she leaned toward him slowly and, keeping her eyes wide open, watching him every instant, she touched her lips to his.

Her mouth was sweet and warm, beckoning him, drawing him in, assuaging his desperate hunger, yet deepening it at the same time.

And Tanner was powerless to resist.

He'd fought too long, too hard. There was no fight left in him. He could only taste and touch and savor, could only open his mouth and press his lips even harder against hers, surrendering and conquering at the same time.

But even that wasn't enough, just as he'd known it wouldn't be. He wanted more. And more. He bore her back onto the bed, his mouth still locked with hers, his body clamoring for equal time. His shoulder ached, limiting what he could do, bludgeoning him with reality, and for an instant he pulled back.

But Maggie still looked at him, still beckoned him. She lifted a hand and lay it against his cheek, stroking his two-day-old beard softly. Her thumb ran lightly across his lips. "Robert, stop fighting it. Come to me."

Some needs were too great, some aches too deep. If she was willing—if even knowing the worst of him, she still wanted him—he couldn't say no.

Her small nipple erect beneath the cotton begged to be tasted. He touched it with his lips.

She shivered. "Yes, Robert. Yes!" Then, instead of holding herself still and compliant, she lifted her hands and slid them down to skim along his sides, to trace the line of his ribs, to brush lightly across his chest. The feel of her fingers on his bare skin was like fire, burning and arousing.

He slid callused fingers under the hem of her shirt, drawing it up so he could see her breasts, so he could watch them peak and see the way they trembled as he touched them gently, as he bent his head and laved them with his tongue. He wished his shoulder didn't hurt so much. He wished he had full use of both his arms and hands to give her all the pleasure he'd dreamed of giving her.

But he didn't have a long time to wish or to concentrate on his hurts. Maggie was sitting up now, pressing kisses against his chest, touching him lightly with her nails, then with her tongue. She set off tremors that centered his passion, his need for her.

"Maggie! Don't! You're going to—"

She stopped, her hands still against his chest as she looked up into his eyes. "You don't like it?"

"God, yes, I like it. It's going to... I'm going to..." He gave a shaky half laugh, half sob. "I like it way too much. We gotta slow down."

She smiled, a catlike, enigmatic smile. "So we'll slow down."

She leaned forward and pressed a kiss against first one of his flat nipples, then the other, then she splayed her hands against his chest and he fell back, at the same time reaching for her with his right arm to draw her on top of him so that she straddled his thighs.

The shirt had slipped down again and he pushed it up. Maggie grasped it by the hem and pulled it over her head in one sensuous movement, then tossed it aside. Then she settled against him again, still smiling, her breasts bare to his gaze.

He couldn't stop looking, couldn't stop touching. There was a fine tremor in his fingers as he grazed the peaks of her breasts, as he made her shiver, as he made her smile.

He remembered the first time he had seen her: she had been looking down at him like this. She hadn't been smiling then; she'd been worried, concerned. Caring.

He saw that care in her eyes now, along with the smile. It made his heart lodge in his throat. No woman, not even Clare, had looked at him quite that way before—as if he were everything she'd ever hoped for.

He wasn't. He knew that. So did she.

She had to know. But just now, he needed to pretend. Just for the space of a few moments, a few hours, he wanted to be that man for her.

Again his fingers lifted to touch her, to trail lightly across her breasts, to draw a line down the center of her, slowly and deliberately, rough calluses against silken soft skin. Down, down, until at last, well below her navel, they reached the thin bit of material that were her panties.

His mouth crooked in a grin. He'd never known schoolteachers wore such scandalous panties.

Whenever he'd imagined undressing Maggie MacLeod, and despite his best intentions he'd done his share of it—why else would he have so many scars from mending fences this year?—he'd always stripped away her sweaters and jeans, her blouses and skirts to find serviceable, no-nonsense, white cotton underwear. Schoolteacher underwear.

Not underwear like this.

Never in a million years would he have imagined Maggie in panties that were no more than this scrap of peach-colored lace.

He swallowed, contemplating them and the woman who wore them, this woman who had tempted him beyond his endurance, who was more mysterious and more desirable than all the other women he'd ever met. She sat very still, watching him, waiting for him to make another move.

He couldn't wait. He slipped his fingers beneath the elastic. The back of them brushed lightly against the smooth, warm skin of her belly. The tips touched the soft curls at the apex of her thighs. His fingers gripped the lace and drew it down. Maggie moved to accommodate him, to let him draw the panties down her legs, wriggling free of them. Then coming back to straddle him again, she slid her own fingers down his chest to feather across his abdomen, to slip beneath the confines of his briefs.

She touched him. One simple touch and he almost lost control. He'd waited so long, daydreamed so much. He'd felt it in his mind a thousand times before—and a thousand times he'd never come close to imagining the reality of her hand on him. It was soft, gentle, feather light. It teased, it tantalized, it tormented. And then it grew bolder, firmer.

"Mag-gie!" Her name was a hoarse exhalation of breath, strangling him. His fingers sought her warmth, her moisture. He saw her bite her lip as he teased her, opened her. She grasped his briefs and tugged them down and he lifted his hips to make it easier for her.

And then he was free, the cool morning air touching his heated flesh as it ached for her to touch him, to stroke him again, to let him into the warmth of her body.

She was ready for him. He was sure of it, could see it, could feel it. He needed to do one thing, though, first.

"Maggie! In my jeans. My wallet."

She frowned, then seemed to realize what he was asking for. She reached down and snagged his jeans off the floor, got out his wallet and gave it to him.

With fumbling fingers Tanner took out the foil package he'd bought in anticipation of the wet-T-shirt contest.

"Show me how," Maggie whispered.

He sucked in his breath. "Like this." Then he shut his eyes as she did it, struggling desperately for control. He was right on the brink, and she'd barely finished when he muttered, "Now! Let me in! Please, Maggie. I can't wait any longer."

Maggie eased herself up. Her hair fell forward, obscuring her face, as with both hands this time, she drew him toward her, guiding him. He nudged against the very center of her, felt her warmth, her welcome. He bit his lip.

"There," he muttered. "No. Yes. Yes. There."

"Help me," Maggie whispered, and Tanner's hand came to meet hers, seeking, finding, easing him in.

"Yes." It was a hiss through his teeth. Sweat beaded his forehead as her tightness began to close around him. He drew her down, thrusting upward as he did so, needing to be inside her—a part of her at last. She tensed. He felt a sudden barrier, stopped, and then couldn't stop any longer.

His hips surged up to connect them completely. With one hand he touched her breasts and teased her nipples, while with the other he began a gentle exploration of the petal softness at the juncture of her thighs. He smiled as his touch made her writhe and squirm. He gloried in the heightened pink of her cheeks, in her lips, full with the passion of arousal.

She moved more quickly now, and Tanner moved with her, caught in a storm of longing he'd never before experienced, captured by a woman he didn't understand, sensing a completeness he'd never known before, but wanted to know again and again.

He felt Maggie's body contracting around him, felt her shudder and tremble and grip him for all she was worth. "Oh! Oh, Robert!"

And he surged into her one last time, spending his passion within her, then sank back onto the mattress, shattered, and gathered her against his chest.

He didn't know how long they lay like that. He felt her heart thundering against his, stroked her back with still-trembling hands. Maggie nestled her head in the curve of his neck and shoulder. Then, as her breathing slowed, she lifted her head and raised her body slightly away from Tanner's chest to look down at him and smile.

She brushed his hair off his forehead.

She traced the line of his brows, trailed a finger down his cheek, tickled the corner of his mouth, making his lips curve into a smile.

She kissed his nose.

"I love you," she said.

And Tanner closed his eyes and hung on to the moment, knowing all too soon it would be gone. He couldn't pretend any longer.

His time had run out.

Eight

It was a long time since he'd gone down the road. Too long. He should've left the Three Bar C sooner. Four years was too long to stay in one place. It made a man lazy, soft.

It was wide open spaces a man really needed. A pickup, a trailer, horses, a saddle. Those were the things that mattered. Nothing else.

Better not even to bother saying goodbye. Who knew? Maybe he'd see them all again someday. Or maybe not.

Tanner drew a deep breath, then let it out slowly, felt the cool night breeze on his arm as it rested on the door of his truck. He was doing the right thing. The only thing.

He'd let Maggie breach his final defense. He had nothing left.

With luck she wouldn't realize he was gone until morning. He could be a couple of states away by then. Not that he expected she'd send out an APB on him. Hell, when she thought about it, she'd be thanking her lucky stars she'd made such a narrow escape.

And it wasn't as if anybody else would care. Ev and Billy were a pair. They'd be fine without him. And Andy— Andy for whom he'd left a note saying, "You've got what it takes to be foreman"—Andy would be thrilled.

There was Abby, of course. But he'd stopped at the cemetery as he'd driven past. It was almost pitch-black, only a sliver of moon hanging in the canopy of stars, but Tanner had made his way unerringly until he came to stand by the granite marker at Abby's grave.

"I tried," he said after a moment. "I did the best I could. And if it isn't good enough for you, I'm sorry. The way I see it, I had a choice: I could fail you now or fail Maggie later."

He didn't wait around to see if Abby might say something from on high. He got back in his truck and headed south.

It didn't take him long to realize that going down the road was different this time. The anticipation was gone, the eagerness to see new places, try new things.

It would come back, he told himself. It had been four years since he'd taken more than a few days off; he would need a little while to adjust.

He wasn't in any hurry to find another job. There was money enough to get by until more work was available in the fall, so he just drifted around. He visited some old friends in LaJunta; he dropped in on an old rodeo traveling partner who had a little spread near Farmington. He left his horses and the trailer there, figuring to pick them up in early fall. Then he headed back north as far as Cheyenne for Frontier Days to watch his brother, Noah, ride.

"Son of a gun!" Noah exclaimed when Tanner knocked on his motel-room door. He reached out and dragged his brother into the room, where five other cowboys lounged in chairs and on the beds. "You remember Tanner, don'tcha? What're you doin' here? I stopped in at your place to see you on my way down. They said you'd quit." Noah looked as if he didn't quite believe it.

"I did."

"Come on. Let's walk down by the pool." He steered Tanner back out of the room and toward the swimming pool. "What the hell'd you leave for? Thought you loved that damned ranch? Couldn't even pry you loose to come down to Cheyenne last year."

"I had work to do last year."

Noah lifted a dark brow. "Ranch learn how to run itself in the meantime?"

"I got fed up. You heard Abby died..."

Noah nodded. "Yeah, I meant to call and tell you I was sorry. But, hey—" he grinned "— she gave you a hell of a replacement. That Maggie's a good-lookin' gal."

"You talked to her?" The words were out of Tanner's mouth before he could stop them.

"Sure. Had dinner with her as a matter of fact. We went to that good little place down in Kaycee."

"You took her out?"

"Sure. Why not?" Noah gave his best imitation of a leer. "When have I ever passed up a pretty woman?"

"As long as having dinner with her is all you did!" Tanner said tightly.

"Ah, like that, is it?" Noah flopped down in one of the lounges and grinned up at his brother. "Open your mouth."

"What?"

"I want to see the hook."

Tanner gritted his teeth. "It's not like that. I just know what you're like—and I don't want you messing around with Maggie. She's a lady."

"Reckon you messed around with her."

Tanner reached down and grabbed his brother by the front of his shirt, dragging him to a sitting position. "We were not 'messing around!'"

Noah looked at him, shaken, then gave him a faint grin. "Whatever you say, big brother." He eased Tanner's fingers away from his shirtfront and swung his feet around so he sat with his forearms resting on his knees. He looked up at Tanner, his expression serious. "I don't get it. She looks stricken every time she talks about you. You practically punch me when I even mention you gettin' together with her. What's goin' on?"

"Nothing."

"Look me straight in the eye and tell me that again," Noah said. It was what their father always used to say to them when he suspected a less-than-truthful reply. Tanner had never been able to lie to his father. He didn't find it much easier to lie to Noah.

"She thinks she loves me," he muttered.

Noah gave a low whistle. "Heavy stuff."

"Yeah."

"Do you think you love her?"

"I try not to think about it!"

"Ah. Yeah, I know how that works." Noah grimaced, and Tanner remembered that for plenty of years his brother had fancied himself in love with Lisa Pickney, a tawny-haired barrel racer who hadn't been interested in him. In the end, all Noah had been able to do was try not to think about it.

"Anyway, it doesn't matter if I do or not," Tanner said finally. "I'm not getting married again."

"Why not?"

"You remember what happened with Clare."

"Yeah, so? Maggie's not Clare."

"But I'm me."

Noah scratched his head. "Whatever that means. It's too deep for me, big brother. Still, I think you're nuts. I sure as hell wouldn't be runnin' the other way if I had a looker like that thinkin' she loved me."

"You'd get married?"

"If it was a girl like Maggie."

There was nothing Tanner could say to that. He shrugged. Noah regarded him curiously, as if he might be able to understand what drove his brother if only he looked long enough. Tanner could have told him not to bother.

"I just need a change," he said finally. "I thought I might go out and see Luke after you win Cheyenne." He managed a grin.

Noah grinned back. "Yeah...when I win Cheyenne. Well, a guy can hope. Be a good idea, you goin' out to see Luke. I saw him a while back. He drove up to Santa Maria when I was there for a rodeo. He, Keith and Keith's girl. But you better go quick. They're leavin' for location in mid-August, I think."

"Location where?"

"Don't know. It's a western, he said. One of those gutsy hell-bent-for-leather types that are making a comeback. Or at least Mallory hopes they are. Might be New Mexico or Texas. Hell, it might be Spain for all I know. Luke gets around."

"Maybe I'll go with him." Spain might be far enough away to get red hair and green eyes out of his mind, Tanner thought as he stretched out on one of the lounges.

"You oughta go see Clare."

Tanner sat bolt upright. "Why the hell should I do that?"

Noah shrugged. "So's you can get on with your life. Hell, the way I see it, brother, you're still married to her."

"I am not still married to her! In many respects," Tanner added in a low voice, "I don't think I ever was."

"Maybe. Maybe not. But I'll tell you one thing, you're a damned fool to throw away a chance with a woman like your Maggie."

"When did you start givin' marital advice?"

"About the time you stopped having the sense God gave a goose."

"Well, if you're going to spend the rest of the week giving me advice like that, I think I'll skip staying around to see you ride."

Noah smiled and stretched his arms above his head, wincing as his muscles complained. "I've said my piece. Now it's your turn. You got to think about what I said."

Tanner thought about it more than he would have liked. Though Noah never brought up Maggie again, it was as if she was right there with them for the rest of the week. There were pauses in the conversation, occasional periods of silence that were somehow filled with memories of her, visions of her. Tanner was glad when the week was over.

"I tried to win for you," Noah said. He was nursing a black eye, courtesy of his own flying fist. But he was standing in the pay line.

"You didn't do so bad." Tanner said. "Made the short round. Finished third. Pretty respectable, I'd say."

"I do what I can," Noah said modestly. "You leavin' now?"

"Uh-huh." Tanner shook his brother's hand. "Reckon I'll see you sometime. Where you gettin' your mail?"

"Durango." He gave Tanner the box number.

"I'll drop you a line, let you know where I end up."

"Do that." Noah hung onto Tanner's hand a bit longer. "Tell you what I'd rather have you send me."

"What's that?"

"A wedding invitation."

Fortunately, Luke didn't know about Maggie. And if he was surprised to see his brother turn up on his Southern-California doorstep early one August morning, he gave no sign.

"I'm not...interrupting anything?" Tanner asked as Luke, looking bleary-eyed and wearing only a pair of shorts, stepped back to let him in.

One corner of Luke Tanner's mouth lifted. "Think I've got a bedroom full of starlets, do you?"

"Maybe I was hoping." Tanner tossed his duffel bag on the floor and looked around.

Luke's house, a Spanish-style two-story stucco only feet from the wide white sand of the South Bay, was a far cry from the sort of place Tanner was used to. And if the house wasn't enough, the silver Porsche in the driveway and the customized Harley next to the back door attested to his brother's affluence and fast-lane life-style.

"Well, I'm sure I can find you someone suitable," Luke said after a moment. "Just let me know what you have in mind."

But the only thing Tanner had in his mind was Maggie. Everywhere he went, there was Maggie. Before he'd spent the week with Noah, he hadn't been able to forget her. Noah, having seen her and formed his own opinions, made it impossible to forget her. But even the sights and sounds of Southern California didn't seem to be able to blot her out of his head.

"I need some sleep," he told Luke, who obligingly pointed him in the direction of a bedroom.

But sleep brought dreams here just as it had everywhere else. And the dreams brought Maggie.

Luke didn't ask him any questions. He took Tanner to the set with him, to parties with him, to the beach and even down to Mexico for a few days of deep-sea fishing. He introduced Tanner to a bevy of beautiful women, most of whom stared and simpered and were fascinated with the notion that he was "a real cowboy."

Tanner threw himself into everything Luke thought up, hoping that it would occupy his mind, but somehow there was always a part of that mind wondering at every moment what was happening back on the Three Bar C, whether Andy was coping, whether Ev and Billy were well, whether Maggie was remembering him the way he remembered her.

Finally, after three weeks and no improvement, Tanner decided it was time to move on.

"You don't have to go," Luke told him. "I'm off for Utah on Monday for the new movie, but you can stay in the house as long as you want."

But staying in one place, even such a single man's paradise as Luke's version of Southern California, wasn't going to solve Tanner's problem. Apparently play of any kind wasn't going to solve it. He needed to get back to work.

Haying wasn't any cowboy's idea of a dream job. It was a measure of Tanner's desperation that when his friend Gil, the rancher near Farmington, said, "Don't suppose you'd like to help with the haying, would you?" that he practically jumped at the chance.

Gil looked at him, taken aback. "Should I call the doctor?" he asked his wife.

Jenn shook her head. "Not for this kind of sickness."

"I'm not sick," Tanner said flatly.

"No," Jenn agreed complacently. "You're in love."

"Why the hell would you say a thing like that?"

Jenn smiled. "I know the signs. Moody, depressed, can't eat or sleep. If California couldn't snap you out of it, you're in pretty bad shape, Tanner. And when you actually agreed to help with the haying, well—" she shrugged "—there isn't any doubt."

"I just want to help out an old friend," he muttered. "Even if the old friend has a nosy, interfering wife."

Jenn laughed. "Whatever you say, Tanner. Whatever you say."

But haying, however tedious, hard, hot and monotonous it was, didn't help either. After a week and a half, he was no closer to forgetting Maggie than he'd ever been. It was because it didn't sufficiently occupy his mind, Tanner decided. He needed a challenge.

"I'm goin' up to Durango next week and ride a bronc," he told Gil.

"Are you nuts? You haven't rodeoed in years. You'll wreck your knee. Or dislocate your shoulder again. Or break your neck. Then again—" and here Gil, who had come to believe all Jenn's preposterous speculations, looked at Tanner closely "—maybe that's what you want?"

"Don't be an ass," Tanner grumbled. "I signed up a couple of weeks ago. Figured if I didn't want to, I could turn him out. Are you coming?"

"To watch you get bloody and broken? No, thanks."

So Tanner went by himself.

"You're coming back after, aren't you?" Jenn asked him.

"If Noah's there, I'll probably go down the road with him a spell—"

"Check out a few hospitals," Gil put in dryly.

"Thanks for your confidence," Tanner said in a sour tone. He got into his truck. "You don't mind keeping the horses and trailer awhile longer?"

"We'll put it on your tab." Gil grinned.

Tanner gave him an answering grin. "I reckon you owe me for all that haying."

"That was therapy," Gil said. "I oughta have charged you. Would have, 'cept it didn't do much good, did it?"

"Not yet," Tanner said heavily. "See you around."

Noah was in Durango. He rode and won. Tanner rode respectably. He got sore, but not bloody. His shoulder stayed in place. His knee didn't cave in.

"Not too bad for an old man," Noah told him afterward over a beer. "You serious about traveling with me for a spell?"

"Yeah." He was. Because riding took total concentration. For eight seconds he hadn't thought of Maggie at all. It was a start.

Going down the road with Noah was serious business. They traveled the length and breadth of all the western states, hopped a plane to someplace in Alberta one Thursday night, flew back to Albuquerque the following evening, got in the truck and drove again after the rodeo. Tanner did them all, praying that his knee would endure, that his shoulder wouldn't slip. It was insane. Unlike Noah, he had no possibility of contending for the NFR. It was just another form of therapy, another way of trying to fill his life, to forget the Three Bar C and Ev and Billy and, most of all, Maggie. It was just a little more drastic than anything he'd attempted yet.

He tried not to moan when he got up in the morning. He tried not to groan when he got out of the truck after hours on the road. The only time he balked was when Noah said they were going to Bluff Springs.

"It's not a big deal," Tanner argued. "You can miss it."

"I'll be damned if I'll miss it. I drew Haverell's Hotshot."

Tanner understood. Hotshot was an NFR bronc. Any cowboy who drew him would be a fool to turn him out and lose a chance at an almost-sure win, especially a man who was currently eleventh in the standings like Noah. It was a long time till November. A lot of horses. A lot of miles. A lot of rides. And you never knew from one day to the next what would happen.

Most of the time you were fine. Sometimes, as Tanner knew all too well, you weren't. So you hoped. You drove. You flew. You rode. And you took every day as it came.

They went to Bluff Springs.

And Tanner hoped he wouldn't run into Clare.

His own horse in Bluff Springs was called Deal's Rampage. "A twister," Noah told him. Tanner's shoulder had survived so far—just barely. It didn't survive his encounter with Rampage. In fact, he felt it pop almost as soon as the chute opened. The horse twisted hard to the right, ducking his head, spinning, and Tanner, as he hung tight, couldn't stand the strain.

Clutching his arm against his stomach, he made his way out of the arena.

"Want me to call the doc?" Noah asked him. He'd already ridden, had scored an 87, and they didn't have to be in Salida until tomorrow. He was more than willing to look up a doctor. The Emergency Medical Technicians, too, were standing around looking hopeful.

Tanner shook his head. He gritted his teeth and tried popping his shoulder back in. The pain almost blinded him. A curse escaped his lips.

"Let's find a doc," Noah said.

"You can put it back in," Tanner said. He led the way to the truck, had Noah drop the tailgate, then he lay down on it and let his arm dangle. "Pull it," he commanded.

Noah shuddered.

"Pull it," Tanner said again.

Noah pulled.

Tanner fainted.

"Hello, Tanner." The voice was soft and had just a hint of a southwestern lilt to it.

Tanner blinked again, staring up at tall trees, white clouds, blue sky—and Clare. He frowned, tried to lift his arm to rub a hand across his eyes, felt the pain, remembered what had happened and winced. Carefully he looked around. He was still lying on the tailgate of the pickup, though he was on his back now. He could see Noah over by the fence, working studiously on his rigging, ignoring them. Mostly he could see Clare.

"Russ fixed your shoulder," Clare told him.

Russ. The doctor who'd delivered their baby. The man who had encouraged Clare out of her depression, who'd gotten her interested in something again, who'd helped her achieve it. The man who'd believed in her, supported her. Married her.

Tanner didn't say anything. He couldn't have if his life depended on it.

"We'd brought the boys to the rodeo," Clare went on rather quickly. "I had no idea you were...I mean, I never thought..." She colored slightly and looked away, then back at him again. "Anyway, when you fainted, Noah made them call for a doctor."

"The EMTs?" Tanner asked hoarsely.

"They were busy with a barrel racer. Russ is with them now. He left me to watch you. Can I—can I get you something to drink?"

Tanner shook his head and swung his legs around, trying to sit up. He felt dizzy and disoriented. He didn't want to see Clare at the best of times. He sure as hell didn't want to see her now.

He glanced again at Noah, remembering what his brother had said he ought to do, wondering if Noah had somehow engineered it. At the same moment Noah glanced over at him. Their eyes met, Tanner's bleak, Noah's challenging.

Tanner turned his head.

"It's...been a long time," Clare said finally.

"Yeah."

"You're looking good. Other than the bruises, I mean." She colored again. "It's awkward, isn't it?"

"Uh-huh."

"It always was," Clare said after a moment. "We never much talked."

"No." Tanner stared at the toes of his boots. "My fault, not yours. You talked. I was too young and too dumb," he said finally. "I thought it would all work out without us having to say anything."

It was as much as he had ever admitted to her, and it had come well past the time when it would do any good. But he knew that, no matter what, he had to say it, had to clear the slate between them.

"I was as bad as you," Clare said ruefully. "We had unrealistic expectations. And you had enormous responsibilities, far too many for someone barely twenty. I wanted to help you, but I just became another one. I'm sorry."

"Don't apologize," Tanner said hoarsely. "For God's sake, don't do that! If anybody should be apologizing, it's me. I was . . . I was never there for you. Or—" he swallowed painfully and looked up to meet her eyes "—for the baby. I'm sorry."

Tentatively, Clare reached out and touched the back of his hand. He saw that hers was strong and capable, callused now. A working woman's hand. She had matured just as he had. More, probably. She had moved on, married, had children. He turned her hand and clasped it in his. His eyes blurred. He blinked, waiting until his vision cleared before he dared look at her again.

"So you're a nurse?"

She nodded. "I held you while Russ popped your shoulder back in. I didn't even flinch." She smiled at him.

"Why would you?" he said with a small smile. "I was the one who was hurting."

"You didn't even know it," she reminded him.

They looked at each other for a long moment. He remembered what a lovely girl she'd been. She was still attractive, but somehow what he'd felt for her didn't compare with what he'd come to feel for Maggie. Was it a matter of adolescent hormones versus adult attraction? he wondered.

He hesitated, then had to ask, "Are you happy?"

Clare's gaze flickered toward where the ambulance was parked and then toward a pair of boys now talking to Noah. Then she turned back to Tanner. "Yes."

"Are those your boys?"

"Yes. Dan's nine. Kevin's five."

They were fair like their mother, tall like their father. Tanner wondered what his child with Clare would have looked like. He felt his throat grow tight. He had to swallow twice before he could say, "Good-lookin' kids."

"Thank you." She paused. "Do you have any?"

He shook his head.

"Are you married?"

"No."

"Never? Haven't you ever married, Tanner?" She cocked her head, looking at him with concern.

He looked away. "No."

"Is it . . ." she hesitated "because of us?"

He wanted to lie to her. He couldn't. He shrugged. "I don't think I'm cut out for marriage. I didn't do a very good job of it."

"Neither of us did," Clare said.

"You made a success of this one."

"And you haven't tried." She said it softly, but Tanner could hear the gentle accusation. "That's the one thing I never thought about you, Tanner."

"What's that?"

"That you were a quitter."

"I thought," Tanner said casually to Noah the next morning, "I might head north, see about gettin' a job again. It's almost time for roundup and I sure as hell can't ride broncs."

Clare's husband, Russ, had made that plain yesterday afternoon. He'd been cordial and very professional. He'd asked Tanner about the shoulder, heard how many times it had slipped out and told him he was crazy to think about riding anymore. He'd mentioned surgery and stress exercises, and personal responsibility and adult behavior. Tanner had gotten the point.

But worse than the threat of surgery was the memory of Clare's words. *I hadn't thought you were a quitter.*

He hadn't thought he was a quitter, either. A non-starter, maybe, where Maggie was concerned, but he'd only been protecting her. Hadn't he?

Or had he been protecting himself?

The question was enough to have kept him awake all night, tossing and turning, cursing the pain and then the painkillers that Noah insisted he take.

"Sounds like a good idea," Noah said now. "Where you thinking on goin'?"

Tanner shrugged. "Reckon I'll see what opens up."

If Noah suspected what he really had in mind, he was tactful enough not to talk about it. "We're headin' toward Durango again Monday," he said. "You can pick up your truck."

He stopped in Kaycee for gas and a little reconnoitering. He wouldn't just drive into the Three Bar C without scouting out the lay of the land. Hell, he'd told himself half a hundred times on the drive north that for all he knew Maggie had gotten fed up and packed it in. Maybe she wasn't even on the ranch now.

"Well, how do you like that? Tanner's back!" Rufe at the gas station said. "Where you been, you ol' son of a buck?"

"Here and there," Tanner said, pumping the gas. "Just goin' down the road."

"Back to stay now?"

"Hard to tell. When's the roundup at the Three Bar C?"

Rufe blinked. "You mean you don't even know?"

"Told you, I've been gone. Why? Is somethin' wrong?" Tanner felt anxiety come boiling up.

"Naw, not now. Kid had a rough time for a while, but he said the other day he figured it was the best thing you coulda done for him—tossing him in an' hopin' he'd swim." Rufe grinned.

"Andy, you mean? Slicker?"

Rufe spat on the ground. "That's the one. You don't need to call him that anymore though. Reckon he's earned a new name."

Tanner smiled and finished filling the tank. Well, at least the place hadn't crumbled. And Andy seemed to have earned the locals' respect.

"They started rounding up this week," Rufe said. "Sure they'll be glad to see you, 'specially Maggie. She was always sweet on you."

"Was she?" Tanner wondered and dared to hope.

It looked the same as he drove in. It looked warm and welcoming. It looked like home. And in a few moments he would see Maggie. His heart pounded. His palms felt damp and his mouth drier than the high-plains desert. He parked the truck alongside the house and went up the back steps.

He put his fingers around the doorknob, then stopped. He remembered the first time he'd come to see Maggie here, when he'd belonged and she hadn't. He licked dry lips, then lifted his hand and knocked.

It was a full minute before he heard footsteps. The door opened. Maggie stood in front of him with her glorious red hair and her beautiful ivory skin, with her scattered freckles and her kissable lips. But there was no smile on those lips, no welcome at all. And in her eyes there was none of the joy he'd seen so often, that he'd actually come to expect to see whenever she saw him.

She looked stunned.

It was nothing compared to how he felt himself. Even though he hadn't been able to forget her for almost three months, he still wasn't prepared for the intensity of the longing he felt the moment he saw her again. It was magnetic, the pull he felt toward her. And only the coldness in her eyes and the sight of John Merritt at the kitchen table kept him right where he was.

"Maggie." His voice sounded a little rusty.

"What do you want?" Hers sounded like cold steel.

To hold you, he thought desperately. *To kiss you and love you. To start over and try again.*

"A job," he said. It was all he could think of. He couldn't say what he wanted to say—not now, not when she was looking at him like that, not when Merritt was sitting there looking at him.

"Just drifting through?" she said, her tone hard.

No, damn it, he wanted to yell at her. *I'm back forever! I'm back to stay.*

But he couldn't get the words past his lips. He clenched his fists at his sides and gave a little shrug and a half smile. "More or less." It was wrong, all wrong, and he knew it. He should never have come. He should have known better.

When was he ever going to learn that he didn't know heads from tails in a relationship? Maggie didn't want him there, not after what had happened between them.

He tucked his hands into his pockets and turned away. "Never mind," he said and started down the steps.

"Wait."

He stopped halfway down and turned to look up at her.

"All right. You're on. We ship on the eighth. I'll pay you for two weeks, starting tomorrow. You know where the bunkhouse is."

Nine

There were three other guys staying in the bunkhouse. Andy wasn't there. He'd moved back to the house a couple of months ago, according to Maggie. It was the one bit of information she'd volunteered. Otherwise she'd been as cold and impersonal as a cigar-store Indian.

She didn't seem to feel anything for him. It was as if what had happened between them had happened between two other people completely. She'd turned back to talk to Merritt. There was nothing left.

At least in Maggie there wasn't.

Tanner wished the same was true for him. But if he'd spent half the way back hoping he wouldn't feel a thing and the other half afraid that he wouldn't, he now knew beyond a doubt that he loved Maggie MacLeod.

And he couldn't tell her so. Not when she looked as if she would shoot him between the eyes if he tried. No, that wasn't true. She looked as if she would stare at him as if he were speaking a foreign language, then walk away.

It was just as well Andy wasn't in the bunkhouse when he came in, he thought. He didn't know how Andy would feel about him being back. He didn't know what Maggie had told him about the circumstances under which he'd gone.

The note he'd left had been as noncommunicative as he could manage. He'd written something about wanderlust and moving on, about being sure Andy could handle things.

He'd tried to write a note to Maggie as well, but no words had come. There had been no way to tell her what he felt. And in the end, he'd convinced himself she'd know why he had gone. She knew better than anyone except Clare how bad he was at relationships.

Had she told anyone else? he wondered. Had she told Merritt?

But if Maggie didn't care at all, Andy was delighted to see him. The boy's face broke into a wide grin when he rode up to the barn that evening and spotted Tanner.

"Hey, Tanner! You're back! Fantastic! Have you seen Maggie? Did she tell you about the mare? Did she show you how Grace has grown? Did you see the sheep?"

Tanner let the questions flow over him, basking in Andy's welcome, wishing his sister had given him a tenth of the enthusiasm. But then, he reminded himself, he'd never hurt Andy the way he'd hurt Maggie. He had no right to expect more from her.

"I just got here, Slicker," he said, then grinned. "I hear you don't deserve the nickname anymore."

Andy beamed. "Who told you that?"

"Rufe."

"I hope it's true."

"Rufe wouldn't have said it if it wasn't."

"Well, then, I owe it all to you. You taught me and then let me do it on my own. Not many people would have had that kind of confidence."

Tanner ran a hand against the back of his neck, discomfited by Andy's endorsement of what had been no more than desperation on his part. "I didn't know," he said roughly. "You might have blown it."

"I might have," Andy said. "But so far I haven't. And with you back to help with the round-up, I reckon I won't. You are stayin', aren't you?"

"For the roundup."

"That's all?"

"We'll see," Tanner said.

Andy flung an arm over his shoulders. "Well, come on, we'll go up to the house and have something to eat."

Billy's enthusiasm equaled Andy's. He launched himself at Tanner from the top of the porch. Catching him against his still-sore shoulder, Tanner winced.

"What's wrong?" Andy asked.

"Pulled my shoulder out again a week or so ago." His gaze strayed to Maggie, who was sitting on the porch peeling and dicing apples for sauce. He was remembering the last time he'd hurt his shoulder and how she had spent the night with him. He remembered what had happened after that night, too.

Maggie's face was carefully blank. She kept right on peeling and dicing and didn't even look at him.

"Is it okay now?" Andy asked.

Tanner nodded. "I'll be able to put in a full day's work if that's what you're worried about."

"It's not," Andy protested. "We don't care if you work or not. We're just glad you're back, aren't we?"

"You bet," Billy said.

Maggie didn't say a word.

Tanner wasn't sure whether anyone else noticed that she didn't talk to him all evening or not. There were enough other people around that the conversation never lagged. Stoney and Wes, two of the hands who were sharing the bunkhouse with him, were there for dinner, and Maggie talked at length with them. She talked to Andy about the sheep and to Ev about who would cook what meals. She helped Billy with his math after dinner, and spoke at length on the phone with someone. Tanner didn't know who. Merritt probably, because he wasn't there.

But she never spoke to him. Never even looked at him.

Not until he was leaving. As he was going out the door to head back to the bunkhouse, he spoke to her directly. "You got anything special you want me to do tomorrow?"

Then she looked at him. "Ask Andy. He's the foreman."

As it happened, Andy asked him. The boy had learned a lot over the summer, but he'd never directed a roundup before. And as the days passed and the cattle needed to be rounded up and brought down, he spent a lot of time conferring with Tanner.

"I know it's a lot to ask," he apologized. "I mean, me bein' called foreman, and asking you to tell me what to do, but—"

"I don't mind," Tanner assured him. He was happy to help. It gave him the illusion that he was contributing something, that he wasn't completely wasting his time. He'd never have gotten that feeling if he'd had to depend on just the few encounters he had with Maggie.

Maggie acted as if she didn't know he was alive.

He tried to get Ev to talk, but Ev wasn't talking much, either.

"How've things been while I was gone?" he said the first time he could actually nail Ev down, which wasn't until the evening of the third day he was there.

Ev was putting up tomatoes for winter and he clattered his jars and lids and tongs for a considerable time before answering. He eyed Tanner at length over the tops of his wire-rimmed glasses. "If you'd cared," he said finally, "you wouldn'ta left."

Tanner, who'd been hoping for a casual conversation that he could lead around to finding out a little more about Maggie's attitude toward him, had a pretty good idea of what Maggie's attitude was just from that.

"You're sore I left."

"Oh, hell, no," Ev said, banging the lid on the canning kettle. "Why should I be sore? I figured you was undependable all along. Never could understand why Ab trusted you."

"That isn't true," Tanner said quietly. "You trusted me as much as she did."

Ev turned and glowered at him, hands on his hips, chin jutting over the top of his tomato-stained white apron. "So I'm a fool, too."

"I couldn't stay," Tanner said finally. He traced a line on the linoleum with the toe of his boot.

"Yeah, I know. 'Cause you were yellow."

The stark words speared him. Tanner opened his mouth to deny it, but knew he couldn't. "Maybe," he admitted. He rubbed his hand against the back of his neck, trying to ease the tension in his muscles. "Maybe I was."

"So what're you back for now?" Ev demanded.

"Maybe I found some courage."

Ev snorted. "Did you?" He didn't sound as if he believed it for a minute. "And you expect Maggie'll welcome you with open arms?"

"She already didn't," Tanner said tightly.

"Yeah, well, unlike some of us, Maggie ain't no fool."

"No," Tanner said heavily. "She's not."

But he was. He had to be, to keep hoping this way. She certainly gave him no encouragement. He worked long and hard every day, bringing cattle down, sorting them out, teaching Andy how to separate them and shape up the herd for market.

The only reward was the work itself. It gave him a sense of accomplishment that he'd forgotten in the months he'd been gone. He'd missed that, too.

He'd missed the ranching, the planning, the labor, the sense of feeling tired but fulfilled at the end of a hard-working day.

He'd missed taking Gambler into the high country and just looking over the land, watching the colors shift, the shadows shrink, then lengthen. There was no place on earth he'd ever loved the way he loved this land. He'd never realized how tied he'd become to the Three Bar C until he didn't have it anymore. For the last three months he'd been lost. He'd gone down the road with never a thought to what he'd left behind. Now he realized that he'd missed the ranch almost as much as he'd missed Maggie.

And having it now was a bittersweet pleasure at best, for in little more than a week the roundup would be over, he thought as he cooled down Gambler Friday evening before supper. If Maggie hadn't softened toward him by then, he would be no better off than he had been before he came.

In fact, he'd be worse.

"Supper will be in half an hour," Andy told him when he came out of the barn. "Mag's running late tonight. Duncan just got here. He's come to help out."

"Duncan?" That surprised Tanner.

Andy grinned. "It's catching. Ranch fever, Ev says we've got. Dunc came back a couple of times after you left in the summer. He's turning into a pretty good hand."

Tanner's mouth quirked into a grin at Andy passing judgment on anyone's ability as a hand. "I'll take a look at him tomorrow," he promised.

"Do that. You want to play Scrabble with us after supper?" Andy asked eagerly, then his expression took on a downcast turn and he shook his head. "I suppose you're goin' into town with Wes and Stoney and Jim?"

As a matter of fact, Wes had invited him to come along that morning. All three of the younger men were looking forward to a Friday night in Casper. Tanner told himself he'd probably be better off if he took them up on it. He'd certainly get a warmer welcome at any bar in Casper than he would in Maggie's living room.

"I'll play Scrabble," he said. It was what amounted to a last-ditch effort. Maybe she would talk to him, give him an opening, and after the game he could suggest that they take a walk.

The first part of his hoped for scenario actually came to pass. Maggie did speak to him.

"I thought you didn't like games," she said, fixing him with a hard stare as he came in the door and approached the table where she and Andy and Ev were sitting, the Scrabble tiles spread out before them.

"A man has the right to change his mind," Tanner said. He smiled at her, hoping for an answering one. She looked down at her tiles. He took the seat opposite her, stretched out his legs and collided with hers. Hastily Maggie pulled back.

"Hey, Tanner," Billy said from where he was sitting with Duncan on the floor. "Duncan's teachin' me about gravity and magnets and stuff. You wanna see?"

"After, okay, sport? Andy tells me you're helping out this weekend," he said to Duncan.

"Doing what I can," Duncan replied. He seemed to bear Tanner no ill will. Obviously Maggie hadn't talked to him either. He turned back to Billy and began drawing something on the pad in his lap.

"Well, let's get on with it. Never thought I'd see the day I'd be playin' Scrabble." Ev said it as if it were a dirty word. "Ab an' me used to play poker. Well, I looked up some words today so's I'd have a chance against all you smart folks. Let's play."

The "smart folks," Tanner figured out pretty quickly, didn't include him. He wasn't verbal at the best of times, and this wasn't one of those.

But it would have helped if he'd had some notion of what he was doing. As it was, he might have fared just as well if the tiles were in Greek.

He just watched Maggie. He remembered the way she'd looked the night he'd come upon her in the field delivering the calf. He remembered the way she'd felt when she'd surprised him as he came out of the creek. He remembered the way she'd welcomed him into her arms, into her body when—

"Damn it, Tanner," Andy said. "I said it's your turn."

"Huh? Oh, er, right." He stared blindly down at the tiles before him, his body tight, his mind shattered. Desperately he shoved some tiles onto the board.

"There."

Andy frowned. Ev scratched his head. "What's that?"

-*"Guppy,"* Tanner said. "It's a fish." At least he thought it was.

"Guppy has two *p*'s in it," Maggie said.

He blinked at her, busy contemplating her lips, remembering their taste.

"You misspelled *guppy,"* she said sharply.

"Oh." Hot blood rushed up his neck into his face. He retrieved his tiles and tried again. All he could think of then was *puck,* but he didn't have a *k,* so that was out. He shoved the tiles around this way and that.

"Ain't there a time limit?" Ev complained. "You're takin' forever."

"Fine," Tanner snapped. He shoved a pair of tiles into place, settling for *up,* which netted him a whole four points. But given his current state of mind, he knew he ought to be glad he'd thought of that.

He tried to catch Maggie's eye whenever she looked up. She never looked his way. He tried to make small talk.

"So, how're the sheep doin'?" he asked.

"I need to concentrate," she said.

Tanner sighed, fidgeted, adjusted his jeans. "You're doing a lot better than the rest of us without concentrating," he said gruffly.

She didn't answer him, just laid her tiles out neatly, then shoved her hair out of her face and leaned her chin in her hand, waiting. Tanner stared at her, fascinated.

"Tanner! Damn it, it's your turn again!" Andy almost shouted at him.

One time, by chance, while he was fumbling with his tiles, he glanced up and caught her looking his way. Their eyes met for only an instant, but it was still there—the connection he'd felt from the first moment he saw her. "Maggie." He breathed her name.

Abruptly Maggie pushed back her chair. "This game has gone on forever. I quit. I'm tired," she announced. "I'm going to turn in."

Andy stared at her. "You can't quit. It's the middle of the game. And anyhow, it's only nine o'clock!"

"If you don't want to play Scrabble we can do something else!" Tanner said desperately.

But it didn't do any good. Maggie was already up the stairs.

It was torture. Pure and simple torture. Being with Maggie and not having her, not sharing a smile with her, a few words, the touch of a hand. He should have left.

He couldn't. She was as necessary to him as the air he breathed. He waited every day for some sign that she still felt the love she'd once claimed to feel for him. And every day his fears and his disappointment grew. He'd never worked harder or suffered more in his life. Not even after his son had died and his marriage had failed.

He couldn't count the number of times he watched her from afar and thought, *Please, Maggie. One look. One smile.*

He never got another chance.

He saw her every day, but never alone. She was halfway across a pasture from him or she was coming out of the barn as he was going in. She was at the other side of the kitchen or the other end of the dinner table. And the night before the trucks came to pick up the cattle, when he volunteered to dry the dishes she was washing, she shook her head.

"No, thank you. It's not your job."

"I know that. I don't mind. I like doing dishes!" he lied.

She didn't laugh at the absurdity of his statement. She just took a towel, dried her hands, waved her arm in the direction of the sink and gave him a little bow and smile. "By all means, then, be my guest. I'll call John and discuss what I should be doing for the sale with him."

And she left him with a sinkful of dirty dishes while she went into the living room and talked to John Merritt on the phone.

He didn't think anything could hurt as much as that had.

This is my herd, he wanted to yell at her. *I bred them, I raised them, I took care of them.*

But he knew what she would say in turn. *You left them. You left me. You had no right to come back.*

So he washed the dishes and wound up breaking a glass in the dishwater. He was twisting a rag in the glass so hard that he cut his hand open and watched the blood turn the water red.

It hurt, but not as much as listening to the soft sound of Maggie's voice talking about the herd, the ranch, the future with Merritt.

And then it was over.

Two weeks gone in the blink of an eye. The last of the cattle loaded. The last of the trucks gone.

Tanner stood in the yard and watched until he couldn't see them anymore. Wes took off right after the trucks did, got his pay, grabbed his gear, shook hands all around and headed west.

"We're goin' to a movie," Billy told Tanner. "Me and Maggie and Granpa. Down in Casper." They got in Maggie's little white car. She didn't even look at him as she walked past.

Stoney and Jim and Duncan left next. "We're goin' out an' hang one on with The Perfesser," Jim said, clapping Duncan on the shoulder.

"You want to come?" Stoney asked Tanner.

He probably should—to deaden the pain a little. He shook his head. "Not this time."

"I'll go," Andy said hopefully.

"And sit on the curb all night if they're checkin' IDs?" Duncan said.

Andy sighed and watched their truck as it bounced down the road toward town. "One more year," he muttered, then brightened. "Actually only five more months."

Tanner, looking at him, couldn't ever remember being that young.

They stood together in the waning sun until there was nothing but silence left. "You want to play a game of Scrabble?" he asked Andy.

Andy looked at him, startled, then blushed. "Well, actually I've, uh, got a date. You know Jack Bates's sister..."

"Mary Jean."

Andy grinned. "Yeah. She's pretty cool. She, er, rented a couple of videos and invited me over." He hesitated. "You can...can come if you want."

Tanner smiled ruefully. "Thanks, but I don't think I've quite got to the third-wheel stage yet." But it seemed he was getting close. He turned and started toward the bunkhouse.

"Tanner? What happened between you and Maggie?"

The question stopped him in his tracks. It was the first time Andy had even suggested he knew there was anything wrong. The youth shrugged awkwardly and came toward Tanner.

"I'm not blind, you know. She was hurt bad when you left. Real bad."

Tanner swallowed. "She might've been hurt worse if I'd stayed."

"How? What do you mean?"

Tanner shook his head. "It's none of your business."

"Maybe not." Andy chewed on the inside of his cheek. "Is it hers?"

Tanner nodded.

"So have you told her?"

"Haven't had a chance."

"You've been here two weeks!"

"She won't talk to me."

Andy made an exasperated sound. "Have you tried?"

Tanner, feeling cornered, shifted from one foot to the other, then rubbed the back of his neck. "Aren't you late for your date?"

"Maybe I am," Andy said. He gave Tanner a pointed stare. "And I wouldn't want to hurt Mary Jean's feelings. Not the way you hurt Maggie's." He turned and started toward the house.

"It isn't the same damned thing," Tanner called after him in the growing darkness.

It wasn't. It was a thousand times worse.

She paid them off in the morning. She sat at the kitchen table and wrote out checks, handing them to each of the hands in turn, always with a smile, a kind word and her thanks.

"You did a wonderful job," she told Stoney. "I'll see you next fall, I hope."

"I appreciate your help," she said to Bates. "You've really come through for us all year."

"I can't tell you how happy I was that you were here to help out. Come back next year," she said to Jim.

One by one they thanked her, too, tipped the brims of their hats and went out.

Until only Tanner was left.

Maggie bent her head, ignoring him standing there two feet from her. All her attention was focused on filling out his check. She finished writing her signature with a flourish, tore the check off and held it out to him. Her bright green eyes met his squarely for the first time since he'd arrived two weeks ago.

Tanner ran his tongue over his lips, a million words inside him screaming to get out, a million things he had to tell her, a million feelings he had to share.

"Maggie." His voice was barely a croak.

She pushed back her chair and stood up, her eyes now nearly level with his. She shoved the check toward him again, her impatience obvious. "Your check."

He didn't know what else to do; with nerveless fingers, he took it.

"Thank you, Tanner," Maggie said, her voice flat. "Now goodbye."

Ten

Until he loved, no man was ever lonely.

He'd never understood that until now. Solitude was one thing, Tanner thought, leaning his arm on the open window of the pickup and driving south. Loneliness was something else.

Loneliness was having a damned crater where the pit of your stomach used to be. It was having a constant ache at the back of your eyes, a soreness in your throat, a wild and desperate longing that wouldn't go away.

She'd dismissed him with five words. But two had said it all.

She'd called him Tanner. And she'd said goodbye.

She'd never called him Tanner before, not in all the months he'd known her. Right from the first she'd smiled and called him Robert. Even when he'd protested, had insisted that everyone called him Tanner, still he'd been Robert to her.

He wasn't now.

And it hurt.

God, he'd never realized how much love could hurt. He thought he'd hurt after his divorce from Clare. He didn't know the half of it. Clare had been under his skin. Maggie was a part of his heart.

But he wasn't a part of hers. Not any longer. He'd killed whatever love she'd felt for him. She'd practically shoved the check into his hand. And then, while he stood, rooted, staring at her, she'd flipped her checkbook shut and said, "Excuse me, please. I'm late. I have an appointment for a haircut in town."

And she'd gone.

She brushed right past him out the door, went straight to her car, got in and drove away. Tanner stood in the doorway, stunned.

And what could he do then but leave as well?

He'd packed his gear, hitched his trailer, loaded his horse and headed out. Going over the ridge toward the highway, he'd run into Andy taking some of the cattle back to the north pasture. His riding was easy now, his movements sure. He'd come a long way in the last few months. He'd do fine.

They'd all do fine.

Except him.

Andy stopped him, looked at the trailer, at Gambler's nose poking through the slats, then at Tanner leaning on the steering wheel. "Does this mean what I think it means?" he'd asked.

"Roundup's over," Tanner said with as much nonchalance as he could muster.

"So you're going?" Andy's voice was heavy.

Tanner gave an infinitesimal nod of his head.

Andy just looked at him. "You're a fool."

Tanner didn't have to be told.

* * *

He made it to LaJunta by nightfall. He had friends there. He could stop, rest, eat, sleep. He drove on. If he kept going he could be in Texas before the sun came up.

And what was in Texas?

Nothing.

Everything he loved was behind him. Texas—and the future—stretched out ahead of him, bleak and cold.

Ahead of him there wasn't a town for miles. He couldn't see a ranch, nor a windmill, nor a cow. As far as he could see ahead of him, he was alone.

He'd been alone before. After Clare he'd thought it was what he wanted—to be free, not to care.

But, damn it, he did care. He cared so much it was tearing him apart. He'd never been able to tell Clare how he felt about anything—their marriage, their child, their divorce. He'd always hoped she'd tell him.

And this time when he'd come back, when he'd seen Maggie there with Merritt, all the things he'd wanted to say to her had fled. He hadn't been able to tell her anything, either. He didn't have enough confidence in himself.

And so he'd worked, and bided his time and suffered in silence. And then, because he'd gotten no encouragement, no warmth, no declaration from her, he'd given up, left without talking.

Just the way he had with Clare.

Was he really going to make the same mistake again?

It was dawn when he pulled into the yard of the Three Bar C. There was a light on in the kitchen. Ev, probably. Maybe Andy.

At least Tanner hoped so, because all of a sudden his mouth was dry and his stomach roiled. Having great resolutions for spilling his guts had been fine in the middle of nowhere, but the thought of actually having to go through with them was scary as hell.

He gripped the steering wheel until his knuckles showed white, took a couple of deep breaths that he hoped would steady his frazzled nerves, then got out of the truck.

The kitchen curtains twitched, but he couldn't see who was behind them. He shut his eyes, gathered his courage, opened them again and knocked on the door.

It jerked open almost at once and Maggie, in her robe, her hair now short and shaggy, stared out at him. Her lips tightened. A muscle in her jaw twitched. "Now what?"

"I want a job."

She blinked. "Roundup's over," she said shortly and started to shut the door.

Tanner stuck his boot in to hold it open. She glared at him. He went on, "I know that. I want more than that."

Her eyes widened, then her chin tilted stubbornly. "Andy's my foreman. I told you that."

"Fair enough." He was getting his bearings now, settling in.

"I can't afford to hire any other cowboys except seasonally."

"I don't want seasonal work. I want full-time."

"I have Bates. He's dependable."

"No more dependable than I am."

"I can't—"

"I want you. I love you. Marry me." This last came out in a rush. He didn't mean to simply blurt it out that way. He would have liked a little more finesse, a little more of a percentage that she wouldn't throw him out on his ear. He should have known he'd blow it. He'd never be a talker, not even to save his life.

Maggie stared at him. "What did you say?" Her voice was hollow. Her face was white.

Tanner's was red, and he knew it. And Maggie could see it this time. There was no darkness to hide behind.

There was nothing left at all anymore. He'd laid it all on the line. His body. His soul. His heart.

Over the hill he could hear the faint sounds of cattle. Down by the barn birds were singing. The coffeepot perked and the old mantel clock gave its quarter-hour chime.

Tanner couldn't look at her, could only wait. He shifted his weight, stared at the toes of his boots, at the worn boards of the porch. Then, finally, he lifted his eyes to meet hers, terrified of what he would see.

Her own eyes were downcast. She gave her head a little shake. Then, slowly, she reached out a hand and drew him inside. Her fingers were as cold as the room was warm. He could feel them shaking. Or, he wondered, was the tremor in his own?

He pushed the door shut behind him and stood facing her, their hands still joined. Then she loosed her grip on him and he felt immediately bereft, abandoned. But then her hands came up and skimmed over his sides, brushed across his shoulders and down his arms. She seemed to need to touch him, to be sure he was solid and real.

Then, "You love me?" she whispered. She sounded dazed when at last she looked at him.

He nodded wordlessly, swallowing hard, holding himself still under the brush of her hands.

Her gaze became more intense. "You want to come back to stay. Permanently?"

God, yes. Forever. He nodded again. "If you'll have me," he said, his voice little more than a croak.

"And you want to marry me? Th-that's the job you wanted?" Her voice broke on a half sob, half laugh.

"I want to marry you." He said it again, slowly this time, looking straight at her, offering her his heart with his eyes, offering her all he had been and, with her help, all he hoped ever to become.

And then he saw it. There! In her eyes he saw glowing once more the love she'd given him time and again. The love he'd spurned and scorned and rejected, the love that had scared him and freed him and, finally, brought him home. The love that until now he had always pushed away.

This time he didn't. This time he reached for it, reached for Maggie and pulled her close, bowing his head, feeling the tears sting against his lids as he crushed her hard and fast in his arms. And her arms came equally hard and fierce around him, locking him in so tight that he wondered if he would ever break loose and hoped he wouldn't.

"I never knew . . ." he whispered raggedly. "I never understood—"

"I know. I know."

"I was too much of a fool!"

"You're not."

"Not now, maybe. I was. And I will be again if I don't have you. Please, Maggie. There's so much I want to say, but it's so hard. I want to try. I want to succeed this time. I can't do it without your help. Please, say yes."

And Maggie said, "Yes."

Cowboys don't stay in bed till noon. They don't scandalize old men and young children and their future brothers-in-law. Unless, of course, they're too far gone in love to think straight and redheaded women have enticed them beyond all their power to resist.

But Tanner had driven all night, he'd laid his heart on the line, and when Maggie had taken his hand and drawn him with her up the stairs, he didn't know about all the other cowboys in the world, but he was damned if he was going to say no.

He did manage to protest a little. "What's Ev gonna think?" he whispered worriedly as they crept up the stairs and passed the old man's closed door.

"That you've finally come to your senses," Maggie said and pulled him into her room.

"And Billy?"

"He's too young to care."

"And Andy?"

"Andy's already out with the herd. He'll never know." She halted just outside her door and turned to look at him. "But we'll stop right here if you want to."

Tanner could hardly wait to wipe that impish grin off her face. He pushed her gently through the door and shut it behind them.

Maggie stepped back and lifted her face. She raised her hands and laid them on his chest, then looked into his eyes, her own green ones wide and expectant.

Tanner smiled and bent his head. He was much better at nonverbal communication.

Their loving was by turns gentle and desperate, eager and tentative. They kissed and stroked, gazed and worshipped, touched and teased. And Tanner began to appreciate once more the joy of Maggie's body. But while an appreciation of the physical Maggie MacLeod was where he'd started all those months ago, he found that what he really valued was Maggie's spirit, her soul, her boundless capacity to love.

He wanted to lose himself in her, to know her as intimately as he had once so briefly known her. But, because he really was trying, first Tanner talked.

They were curled together in the quilt on Maggie's bed, her head resting on his chest, his fingers stroking her ear and hair to let their passions cool a bit, let their rampaging hearts slow down.

Finally Tanner lifted his head enough to press a kiss onto the top of hers, then he lay back again and swallowed, trying to decide where to begin.

"I can't believe I'm really here," he said at last, because that more than anything was really what he felt in his heart.

Maggie raised her head and their eyes met. Hers were a warm jade now, with nothing left of the coldness he'd seen in them over the past two weeks. "I can't, either," she said softly. "I never believed you'd come back."

"I had to. Besides, I did come back before," he reminded her.

"But you didn't say anything."

"Merritt was here."

Maggie looked at him horrified. "You mean you would have said you loved me then? Why didn't you? I told you John was a friend."

"I know. But you were looking like you wished I was dead. It seemed like a big mistake."

"You stayed anyway."

"I couldn't leave," he said simply.

Maggie drew her finger down his cheek wonderingly. "Then later, after John left . . . why didn't you tell me?"

"Every time I saw you, you glared at me. If looks could've killed I'd have been six feet under."

"I was afraid . . . of what I felt for you."

Tanner stared. He hadn't thought it had happened to her, too. "Then you know how I felt."

Maggie nodded. "I was afraid I'd betray myself before you left again. I almost did when I gave you that check."

"I wish to God you had."

"But . . . what happened? You did leave. And then you came back. What changed your mind?"

Tanner lifted one shoulder in an awkward shrug. How could he explain what he didn't know for sure himself?

"It was Texas, I guess," he said at last.

"Texas?" Maggie rolled over to lie looking at him, her chin resting on her arms, which were folded across Tanner's chest.

He stared up at the ceiling, remembering how he'd felt out there in the middle of nowhere, when the vastness of a world without Maggie had really hit him.

"It's where I headed when I left. I don't know why, really. I guess because it was there. But the closer I got, the bigger it got—and every bit of it was lonely. It scared me to death." He raised himself up on his elbow and looked at her. "I know how to be alone. Over the years, well, you know I've been alone a lot. After the mess I'd made of marriage to Clare, I thought it was better that way. But the closer I got to Texas, the closer I got to bein' empty, to seeing the rest of my life as nothing but empty. And...I've been empty for so damn long, Maggie. Too damn long." His voice broke, his throat closed. "I just never knew it until I met you."

It was more than he'd said in one breath in years, maybe in his entire life. It might be more than he could ever say again, unless Maggie helped him change. But for what it was worth, it was what he felt.

And Maggie understood. She edged up and kissed him tenderly. It was a long kiss, a slow, thorough, leisurely kiss that began to heat once more his barely cooled blood. But then she stopped kissing him and lay her smooth cheek next to his stubbled one, nuzzling him briefly.

"I thought I'd die when you left after we'd made love," she confided. Her voice had an ache in it that he'd never heard before, and he turned his head to try to see if her expression was as hurt as her words. It was. "I wanted to."

"No," Tanner protested.

"I did. It was awful. The ultimate rejection."

"I didn't mean— I thought I was protecting you!" he said with anguish. "I didn't know what else to do. I sure as hell couldn't resist you. I'd just proved that. And you said you loved me—"

"I did!"

"Though God knows why you should have," he said grimly. "I was a jerk to you. I didn't want you here right from the start. I tried to get rid of you."

Maggie cocked her head, smiling slightly. "Did you?"

Tanner blinked, confused. "Didn't I?" Sometimes now he wondered just what he'd been doing. A corner of his mouth lifted, too. "Is that what Bates would call an approach-avoidance conflict?"

Maggie's smile widened and he noted the tiny dimple at the side of her mouth. "I think that's it."

"Well, whatever you call it, it was a hell of a mess," Tanner said. "I wanted you. Desperately. And I was pushing you away at the same time. I had to. It was pretty damned clear you weren't into one-night stands, and as far as I was concerned, a relationship had no future."

"And now it has." Maggie said the words simply, starkly and with absolute faith.

Tanner shut his eyes and considered the idea. A future. A marriage. He and Maggie together. Forever. And he believed it—perhaps for the very first time.

"It isn't going to be easy," he said.

"I think you've already proved that," Maggie replied dryly.

He grinned. "But you reckon you can bully me into making a tolerable husband anyway?"

"I think you're going to make yourself into a wonderful husband," Maggie told him.

Her confidence startled him. It was so much greater than his own. All the way back home during those hundreds of miles and hours of driving, he'd thought about his hopes, about his fears, about what a marriage would ask of him, about whether he would have the courage to open up, to trust, to try.

And then he thought about Maggie, about her love for him, as deep and abiding as any he could imagine. He thought about his love for her, which seemed new and fragile and untried.

He thought about telling Andy some months ago that the only way to learn something was by doing it.

The same, he supposed, went for loving. And for being a good husband. Maybe even, someday, being a father.

"What about kids?" he asked her suddenly. "Do you want any?"

"Of course I do. Lots of little Tanners. Half a dozen at least."

"Half a dozen?" He looked at her, horrified.

Maggie laughed. "Well, maybe two or three." Then she hesitated. "You want some, don't you?" she asked, as if it had just occurred to her that, given his earlier experience, he might not.

"I do. Very much. I never realized how much until just recently. Until I told you about—about the baby... I'd never talked about him at all. I'd never let myself think about all the things I've missed, that I wanted and was afraid to want. I'd never really grieved."

Maggie slipped her arms around him then, holding him close, kissing him. And the passion he'd kept banked for so long burst into flame. He kissed her back, hungrily, eagerly, fervently.

And then he loved her, fully and completely. He showed her with his hands and his lips and his body the things that he still couldn't find the words to say. And he gloried in her response, in her desire as she met him move for move, in the glow of love that shone in her eyes when together they shattered and at the same time became one.

"Maybe we could try for half a dozen," he said as soon as he could get his breath.

Maggie giggled and slipped her arms around him, hugging him close. "We'll try for a hundred if you want. I love you, Tanner."

He drew back, looking down at her, questioning, worried. "Tanner?" he echoed.

She gazed at him, touched his cheek, smiled. "Robert," she amended, touching her lips to his. "I love you, Robert."

He never corrected her again.

*   *   *   *   *

Watch for Luke Tanner's story in
COWBOYS DON'T QUIT, *the second installment of Anne McAllister's exciting series* CODE OF THE WEST. *It's coming your way this summer— only from Silhouette Desire!*

Get Ready to be Swept Away by
Silhouette's Spring Collection

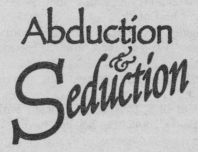

Abduction
& Seduction

These passion-filled stories explore both the dangerous
desires of men and the seductive powers of women.
Written by three of our most celebrated authors, they are
sure to capture your hearts.

Diana Palmer
Brings us a spin-off of her Long, Tall Texans series

Joan Johnston
Crafts a beguiling Western romance

Rebecca Brandewyne
New York Times bestselling author
makes a smashing contemporary debut

Available in March at your favorite retail outlet.

MILLION DOLLAR SWEEPSTAKES (III)

No purchase necessary. To enter, follow the directions published. Method of entry may vary. For eligibility, entries must be received no later than March 31, 1996. No liability is assumed for printing errors, lost, late or misdirected entries. Odds of winning are determined by the number of eligible entries distributed and received. Prizewinners will be determined no later than June 30, 1996.

Sweepstakes open to residents of the U.S. (except Puerto Rico), Canada, Europe and Taiwan who are 18 years of age or older. All applicable laws and regulations apply. Sweepstakes offer void wherever prohibited by law. Values of all prizes are in U.S. currency. This sweepstakes is presented by Torstar Corp., its subsidiaries and affiliates, in conjunction with book, merchandise and/or product offerings. For a copy of the Official Rules send a self-addressed, stamped envelope (WA residents need not affix return postage) to: MILLION DOLLAR SWEEPSTAKES (III) Rules, P.O. Box 4573, Blair, NE 68009, USA.

EXTRA BONUS PRIZE DRAWING

No purchase necessary. The Extra Bonus Prize will be awarded in a random drawing to be conducted no later than 5/30/96 from among all entries received. To qualify, entries must be received by 3/31/96 and comply with published directions. Drawing open to residents of the U.S. (except Puerto Rico), Canada, Europe and Taiwan who are 18 years of age or older. All applicable laws and regulations apply; offer void wherever prohibited by law. Odds of winning are dependent upon number of eligible entries received. Prize is valued in U.S. currency. The offer is presented by Torstar Corp., its subsidiaries and affiliates in conjunction with book, merchandise and/or product offering. For a copy of the Official Rules governing this sweepstakes, send a self-addressed, stamped envelope (WA residents need not affix return postage) to: Extra Bonus Prize Drawing Rules, P.O. Box 4590, Blair, NE 68009, USA.

SWP-S295

is
DIANA PALMER'S
THAT BURKE MAN

He's rugged, lean and determined. He's a
Long, Tall Texan. His name is Burke, and he's
March's *Man of the Month*—Silhouette Desire's
75th!

Meet this sexy cowboy in Diana Palmer's
THAT BURKE MAN, available in March 1995!

Man of the Month...only from Silhouette Desire!

A new series from Nancy Martin

Who says opposites don't attract?

Three sexy bachelors
should've seen trouble coming
when each meets a woman
who makes his blood boil—
and not just because she's beautiful....

In March—
THE PAUPER AND THE PREGNANT PRINCESS (#916)

In May—
THE COP AND THE CHORUS GIRL (#927)

In September—
THE COWBOY AND THE CALENDAR GIRL

Watch the sparks fly as these handsome hunks fall for
the women they swore they didn't want!
Only from Silhouette Desire.

SILHOUETTE®
Desire®
Hearts of Stone

Three strong-willed Texas siblings whose rock-hard protective walls are about to come tumblin' down!

A new Silhouette Desire miniseries by

BARBARA McCAULEY

March 1995

TEXAS HEAT (Silhouette Desire #917)
Rugged rancher Jake Stone had just found out that he had a long-lost half sister—and he was determined to get to know her. Problem was, her legal guardian and aunt, sultry Savannah Roberts, was intent on keeping him at arm's length.

August 1995

TEXAS TEMPTATION (Silhouette Desire #948)
Jared Stone had lived with a desperate guilt. Now he had a shot to make everything right again—until the one woman he couldn't have became the only woman he wanted.

Winter 1995

TEXAS PRIDE
Raised with a couple of overprotective brothers, Jessica Stone *hated* to be told what to do. So when her sexy new foreman started trying to run her life, Jessica's pride said she had to put a stop to it. But her heart said something *entirely* different....

SILHOUETTE... Where Passion Lives

Don't miss these Silhouette favorites by some of our most
distinguished authors! And now you can receive a discount by
ordering two or more titles!

SD#05786	QUICKSAND by Jennifer Greene	$2.89	☐
SD#05795	DEREK by Leslie Guccione	$2.99	☐
SD#05818	NOT JUST ANOTHER PERFECT WIFE		
	by Robin Elliott	$2.99	☐
IM#07505	HELL ON WHEELS by Naomi Horton	$3.50	☐
IM#07514	FIRE ON THE MOUNTAIN		
	by Marion Smith Collins	$3.50	☐
IM#07559	KEEPER by Patricia Gardner Evans	$3.50	☐
SSE#09879	LOVING AND GIVING by Gina Ferris	$3.50	☐
SSE#09892	BABY IN THE MIDDLE	$3.50 U.S.	☐
	by Marie Ferrarella	$3.99 CAN.	☐
SSE#09902	SEDUCED BY INNOCENCE	$3.50 U.S.	☐
	by Lucy Gordon	$3.99 CAN.	☐
SR#08952	INSTANT FATHER by Lucy Gordon	$2.75	☐
SR#08984	AUNT CONNIE'S WEDDING		
	by Marie Ferrarella	$2.75	☐
SR#08990	JILTED by Joleen Daniels	$2.75	☐

(limited quantities available on certain titles)

AMOUNT	$_____
DEDUCT: 10% DISCOUNT FOR 2+ BOOKS	$_____
POSTAGE & HANDLING	$_____
($1.00 for one book, 50¢ for each additional)	
APPLICABLE TAXES*	$_____
TOTAL PAYABLE	$_____
(check or money order—please do not send cash)	

To order, complete this form and send it, along with a check or money order
for the total above, payable to Silhouette Books, to: **In the U.S.:** 3010 Walden
Avenue, P.O. Box 9077, Buffalo, NY 14269-9077; **In Canada:** P.O. Box 636,
Fort Erie, Ontario, L2A 5X3.

Name:_____

Address: _____City:_____

State/Prov.:_____ Zip/Postal Code:_____

*New York residents remit applicable sales taxes.
 Canadian residents remit applicable GST and provincial taxes.   SBACK-DF

Silhouette®
TM